GN00793031

November Lake

Teenage Detective
(The November Lake Mysteries)
Book 2

Jamie Drew

Copyright © 2014 Jamie Drew
All rights reserved.
ISBN: 10: 1503384012
ISBN-13: 978-1503384019

Copyright 2014 by Jamie Drew

This book is a work of fiction. The names, characters, places, and incidents are products of the writer's imagination or have been used fictitiously and are not to be construed as real. Any resemblance to persons, living or dead, actual events, locales or organisations is entirely coincidental.

This eBook is licensed for your personal enjoyment only. This eBook may not be re-sold or given away to other people. If you would like to share this book with another person, please purchase an additional copy for each recipient. If you're reading this book and did not purchase it, or it was not purchased for your use only, then please purchase your own copy. Thank you for respecting the hard work of this author.

Also by Jamie Drew

November Lake: Teenage Detective (Book 1)

November Lake: Teenage Detective (Book 2)

About the author:

Jamie Drew is the author of the 'November Lake: Teenage Detective Series'. Just like, November Lake, Jamie Drew has been a real police officer and has solved many crimes and mysteries in real life.

Jamie Drew now writes full time and is currently working on further 'November Lake' mysteries.

You can contact Jamie Drew by emailing: LakeNovember@aol.com

November Lake: Teenage Detective

The Reappearing Knife

The Death at Hook Inn

Splitfoot & The Dead Girl

The Mystery of November Lake & Kale Creed

The Reappearing Knife

November

"To my horror, every morning when I wake up, I discover that someone has crept into my house and left a butcher's knife lying on the carpet outside my bedroom door," he said.

Now how could I ignore a statement like that? Even though Kale and I had solved the mystery of Veronica Straw, Sergeant Black had warned us one last time to keep ourselves out of trouble.

"I don't think you two hear so well," he had barked at Kale and me as we stood in the dark outside Wendy Creswell's cottage and watched Ethan Cole being placed into the back of a police van.

"We just caught a killer," Kale reminded our sergeant.

"And solved a missing person's enquiry," I said in the defence of Kale and I.

"I couldn't give a damn if you just discovered who Jack the Ripper was..." he huffed.

"His name was..." I started.

"Shut it!" Sergeant Black warned me. "You and Creed just don't get it, do you?"

"Get what, sarge?" Kale asked right back.

"You just can't go charging all over the place like Cagney-and-bleeding-Lacey on speed," he fumed.

"Who?" Kale raised an eyebrow and looked at me.

I shrugged my shoulders. "I think they were from some old cop TV show."

Kale looked at Sergeant Black's silver hair. "Was it like shown on TV in the sixties or something?"

"Don't push your luck, Creed, or I'll bust you back five weeks," Sergeant Black warned, jabbing Kale in the chest with his finger.

The police van pulled away from the kerb, lights illuminating the night sky in pulses of blue and red. Scenes of Crime officers dressed in white papery suits made their way into the back garden where they would start to excavate the grave of Veronica Straw. I looked back at Sergeant Black and just wished that he would give Kale and me some credit for finding her killer. But there was a small part of me that could understand his point of view. We were just new recruits and had only been at training school five weeks. I guess he feared Kale and I might go and get ourselves involved in something we couldn't handle and get hurt, or worse. Perhaps Black did just have our best interests at heart.

"It won't happen again," I said, fearing that he was fast losing his patience with us. I didn't want to be kicked off the force so soon. I wanted to stay so I could investigate the murder of my father.

"You bet it won't happen again, Lake," he said, looking at me. "I want you and Creed to stay apart for the rest of your vacation. If I find out you've so much as sent each other a text, I'll be over the pair of you like a rash. Now get yourselves back to Bleakfield, keep away from each other, and keep out of trouble."

So Kale drove us back to Bleakfield. We sat together in silence as if we were too scared to speak to each other. It was like Sergeant Black was watching us somehow. Pulling up outside my rented rooms, I looked at him through the hazy morning light that reflected off the windscreen. His chin was covered in stubble and he looked tired. "I guess I'll see you next week," I said.

"I guess," Kale said, looking forlorn.

There was a long silence.

"What?" I asked, sensing he wanted to say something but couldn't find the right words.

He looked at me, then away again. "It doesn't matter," he said, leaning across me and opening the car door so I could climb out.

I stood and watched him. Before he drove away, he looked back at me. I half expected him to wave, but he didn't, he just turned his head and looked front. I made my way up the steps and into my flat. After showering and wrapped in a dressing gown, I made a pot of tea and sat in the chair by the window. I watched raindrops race each other down the windowpane. Usually, I enjoyed my own company, but now I felt lonely. It was a horrible feeling, and one I wasn't used to. I plucked up my iPod and switched it on. I drew my thumb over the screen and selected the track *Time After Time* by Cyndi Lauper. Drawing my knees up to my chest, I closed my eyes, resting my head against the arm of the chair.

It was dark when I woke and the battery had gone flat on my iPod. My neck was sore from where I had fallen asleep curled up in the chair. Getting up, I dropped my iPod into its charger. My mobile phone was flashing in the darkness. I scooped it up. There was a text message from Kale.

Hey November, wot u up 2?

My thumb hovered over the screen. Should I text Kale back? I wanted to. But Sergeant Black had warned us to keep apart. Trouble and mayhem seemed to follow close behind when Kale and I were together. I couldn't risk getting into trouble with Black again.

I switched off my phone and went to bed.

Kale

I headed up the stairs to my rooms. I pushed open the door and stepped into the sea of upturned Coke cans and cheeseburger wrappers that covered the living room floor. The thought of eating on my own again was depressing, so I turned around, headed back down the stairs, and left my flat. Pulling the collar of my coat up about my throat, I walked the short distance into town. I would rather sit alone in Mickey-D's and eat my breakfast than sit at home alone. At least there were other people, even if they were strangers. It was company of a sort. I munched slowly through my breakfast. I tried to take as long as possible, just small bites, putting off the inevitable return to my flat and its four walls.

I could only hang out at Mickey-D's for so long before the guy clearing the tables thought I was homeless. I got up and left, taking the long route home through the rain. I tried to push thoughts of November from my head, but it was impossible. She lingered at the back of my mind. We had become friends, and the sudden realisation that we had been banned from communicating had rattled me. And I wasn't quite sure why? November was fun to be with. She was smart and funny. She was exciting. But one thing was for sure, I was pissed off with Sergeant Black for telling us we had to stay away from each other. What was he, my mother? Who was he to choose my friends?

Reaching my flat, I went inside and up to my room. I closed the door and wadded through the ankle-deep crap that covered my floor. I would tidy it up later. Why I bothered I did not know. It wasn't like anyone was going to pay me a visit anytime soon. Bleakfield was miles from my own home and friends. I had only moved to the town to be close to police training school. The only people I knew were those I had met there. And the one true friend I had made in Bleakfield, I was now banned from seeing. Kicking off my shoes, and chucking my clothes onto the bedroom floor, I switched on the radio. I stood in the shower and let the warm water run over me as I listened to Oasis sing the song *She's Electric*.

Dressing in a T-shirt and tracksuit bottoms, I dropped onto the sofa. I switched on the PlayStation and started to play Call of Duty on zombie mode. Every zombie I shot in the face I pretended was Sergeant Black. Having being awake all night, it wasn't too long before I was struggling to keep my eyes open. So, switching off the PlayStation, I lay down on the sofa. I picked up the brick that was my mobile phone. It was nothing fancy like November's. Mine was only valuable because it was so old it was probably considered an antique. With November at the forefront of my mind again, I sent her a short text. I know I had been banned from doing so – but how was Sergeant Black ever going to find out I had?

I feel asleep clutching my phone in my hand, waiting for November's reply.

November

I knew that if I spent the rest of the week hanging out in Bleakfield it wouldn't be too long before I was drawn in Kale's direction. He had already sent me one text and another would follow. The urge to reply to the first was gnawing away at me like an out-of-reach itch. No, I had to get away from Bleakfield or risk getting myself into trouble with Kale again. I didn't want either of us to be kicked out of training school.

But where could I go and what should I do? I hadn't visited my father's grave recently. Not since his death. My father had requested in his will that he be buried in the grounds of a church called the Sacred Heart, which was on the outskirts of a town called Port Haven. I didn't know why that particular church and town, but maybe it had something to do with his past. There was a small hotel named The Hook Inn. It was out of season, so I would have no trouble getting a room. I had stayed there just once before, the night of my father's funeral, and the place had been like a ghost town and that had been during the height of the holiday season.

So, taking a scrap of paper, I sat in the chair by the window and made a list of all the things I could do to keep myself busy over the next week.

Visit Dad's grave at the Sacred Heart.
Stay at Hook Inn
Go shopping
Revise for police exam
Keep away from Kale (although I don't really want to!).

I looked down at the list I had made. My week ahead was planned. I placed the list on the coffee table and went to my bedroom, where I packed a small bag with enough clothes to last me for the next few days. I took my phone and buried it at the bottom, ridding myself of any temptation to message Kale.

Within the hour I was heading out of Bleakfield and toward the town of Port Haven that was nestled amongst the coves further along the coast. Rain spat against the visor of crash helmet, and pelted off my black leather jacket and jeans. My sleek looking motorbike lurched and bounced over the uneven country roads as I left Bleakfield and Kale behind me for the rest of the week. No more adventures – no more mysteries to solve – and no more getting into trouble with Sergeant Black.

I had been riding through the wind and rain for just over two hours when in the distance I could see the spire of the Sacred Heart Church through the leafless trees that lined the roads. Seeing it up ahead made me think of the last time I had been to the church. I had been dressed all in black and standing at the side of my father's open grave. It had been raining that day, too. There had only been a small gathering of people at my father's funeral, just friends from the various police departments he had worked during his career. I had been surprised by this as I'd always believed my father to be a popular and well liked member of the police force. I didn't really know any of them. They all promised to stay in touch, but not one of them did. I guess life just moves on and the dead get forgotten. I hadn't forgotten and never would. I had made him a promise to him that day as he was lowered into the ground. I had promised I would find his killer. That's why, however unfair Sergeant Black's orders that me and Kale should keep apart might seem, it was important that I obeyed it. I couldn't risk being kicked off the force. I needed to stay in it if I ever stood a chance of finding out who had murdered my father.

I rested my motorbike next to the slate wall that surrounded the church and the graveyard. Taking of my crash helmet, I could see there was a narrow path that led through a set of wrought iron gates and amongst the slanting headstones. The church loomed ahead and it looked very old. Some scaffolding had been erected against one side of the spire, as if stopping it from tumbling down. Pulling my coat about me, and my long, blonde hair billowing about my shoulders, I made my way across the graveyard in the direction I remembered my father's grave to be. His headstone was easy to find. It was the only one that didn't look like someone had been leaning against it. It stood straight, and unlike the others, it wasn't broken, smashed, or cracked. But there was something else that made it stand out. My father's grave was the only one that had a small posy of flowers lying on it. They had been placed there very recently, as the flowers still had their petals bright with colour. There was a small, white card attached to the flower stems. I picked up the flowers and read the card. *Miss you, brother. Love, Joseph.* My father didn't have a brother, and I didn't know anyone called Joseph. So, suspecting that perhaps the posy of flowers had been blown by the wind onto my father's grave, I laid them to one side in the grass.

I stood beside my father's grave. With my hands clasped together in my lap, I said, "I'm still looking for him, dad. I'm in the police now, but I guess you already know that as I'm sure you're watching over me. I will find your killer. I won't stop until I get to the truth of what happened to you that day. It's strange because sometimes I get this feeling inside – deep down inside – that there are lots of secrets I have yet to discover. But I will figure out the answers in time. It's just another puzzle, right? That's what you always used to say. Life is just a puzzle that we figure out along the way." I wiped away the tears that were stinging at the corners of my eyes. "I've made a friend. His name is Kale Creed. We're alike in a lot of ways. He loves to figure things out..."

"Are you okay?" I heard someone suddenly ask over my shoulder.

With a gasp trapped in the back of my throat, I spun around to find a man dressed all in black standing behind me.

Kale

I rolled over, my phone spilling from between my fingers and landing amongst the cheeseburger wrappers and old pizza boxes covering my living room floor. Sunlight spilled in through the windows and I covered my eyes with my arm. I felt blindly for the phone, picking it up. Peeking from beneath my arm at it, I checked to see if I had any missed messages from November. There wasn't any. I dropped the phone amongst the litter again and rolled over. She had really taken Black's warning to heart. Could I blame her? November had explained how much she wanted to be a cop, and if she lasted the distance then I knew she would make a great one. She wanted to be one as she believed that working from the inside she would be able to investigate her father's murder. I think November had said her father had been called Thomas Lake. So perhaps if I valued November's friendship as much as I knew in my heart I did, then I should leave her alone for the rest of the week. I didn't want to be the reason she failed police training school.

Dragging myself up, I swung my legs over the edge of the sofa and padded into the bathroom and took a leak. My tongue felt as stiff as an old piece of carpet, so I stuck the toothbrush in the corner of my mouth and left the bathroom for the kitchen. I checked the fridge for milk. What was left in the bottle had gone sour. I would be having my coffee black. I couldn't face another Mickey-D's. I was gonna end up looking like Ronald-freaking-McDonald if I carried on eating takeout. I went to the window and looked out at the dreary sky. It was raining again. The week seemed to stretch out before me like a bleak and featureless road. There must be something I could find to do that didn't involve eating junk food, killing zombies, and... and thinking about the fun I was missing with November. What had I found to fill my life before I'd met November Lake? Oh yeah, I remember now, I had spent it eating junk food and killing zombies.

After showering and changing into fresh clothes, I went back to my phone. I pretended that I hadn't checked it for messages from November before stuffing it into my trouser pocket. I paced back and forth across my flat. I could always tidy my flat. Nah, I wasn't that bored. Not yet anyway. What was the time? Instead of checking the watch strapped to my wrist, I checked the clock on the front of my phone: 11:10. While I had it in my hand, I thought that perhaps I should check it for any missed messages. My mother could have tried to call.

Still no message from November nor my mother.

Blowing out my cheeks and pacing the room again, I went back to the window.

Still raining.

I know, I would take a drive out into the country. Get some fresh air, blow the cobwebs away. Clear the mind a bit. Snatching up my keys and throwing on my coat, I left my flat. I climbed into my car and set off toward the coast. The music coming from the radio melted into the background and the sound of rain beating off the windscreen drowned it out. I don't know how long I drove around for, but it was as if I were functioning on autopilot. The scenery whisked past me in a blur, the trees, sky and houses melting into one. I gripped the steering wheel and tried to force myself out of the stupor I had sunken into. It was then I realised I was turning onto the street where November lived. How had I ended up here? I wondered. But in my heart I knew how. I swept passed her apartment. Glancing up at the window where she sat and looked out, there was no sign of her. At the end of the street, I parked. I sat in the car, my fingers strumming against the steering wheel as the rain beat against the roof of my car. I opened the car door to get out, but then quickly closed it again, Sergeant Black's warning now very loud in my ear. I turned the key in the ignition and drove out of the street.

November

"I didn't mean to startle you," the priest said with a smile. "Perhaps I should leave you…"

"No, it's okay," I said. "I was just talking to my father, if that makes sense," I said, looking back at his grave.

"It makes, perfect sense," the priest said, coming to stand beside me. He wore a black shirt and trousers. The only spark of colour was the white dog collar about his throat. "He can hear you, you know."

"I hope so," I said. "I should've come sooner."

"You don't have to come here to speak with your father," the priest said, looking down at the grave.

"No?" I said, glancing sideways at him. He couldn't have been any older than thirty-five. He had black hair and wore glasses. His nose was hooked, but he had a kind look about his face.

"I remember thinking when my own father passed that I didn't have to call him or go visit to speak with him, I could speak to him whenever I wanted to now. Wherever I was, whatever I was doing, I could always tell him my fears, worries, and hopes."

"I've never thought of it like that before," I said, looking back at my father's grave. "It's kind of comforting."

"So stop looking so sad," he said. "I bet your dad doesn't like seeing you look so unhappy."

I looked at him. "Do I look sad?"

"Very," he smiled. I noticed that the priest had green eyes and they almost seemed to twinkle behind his glasses. "Do you want to talk about it?"

"I don't want to be any bother," I said.

"No bother," the priest said, gesturing to a nearby bench beneath a tree. The rain had stopped and the October sun was peeking through the scattered clouds overhead. I followed him to the rickety-looking bench and sat down. "I'm Father Rochford, but you can call me Michael if you like."

Dead leaves scuttled about my boots in the breeze. "I'm November Lake," I smiled.

"Pleased to meet you, November," he smiled back.

There was a pause in the conversation, but it wasn't uncomfortable. I looked up at the orange sun, and let its lukewarm rays caress my face. The weather had been so drab lately, it was wonderful to feel the sun against my skin. I had started to feel more cheerful already. I took my sunglasses from my jacket pocket, perching them on the bridge of my nose.

"I get the feeling that it's not just visiting your father's grave that has made you so sad?" Father Rochford asked me.

Tilting my head and looking down at my hands resting in my lap, I said, "I think I'm being unkind to my friend, but I don't have a choice."

"We all have a choice to make from time to time," Father Rochford said.

"It's a choice between my friend and my career," I said looking at him.

"Is this friend your boyfriend?" he asked me.

I shook my head. "No, Kale isn't my boyfriend. We're just friends but I like him very much. He is a good friend, my only friend."

"So where does your career fit in?" the priest asked me.

"Kale and I are both police officers," I started to explain.

"You're a police officer" he asked, eyebrows raised behind his glasses. "You look far too young."

"I'm in training, not a proper copper yet, as my sergeant likes to keep reminding me," I said. "Kale is a probationer, too."

"So if you and your friend Kale are both police officers, where's the problem?" Father Rochford frowned.

"Kale and I keep getting ourselves into trouble," I tried to explain. "Our sergeant thinks we are a bad influence on each other. We are on leave this week and the sergeant has warned us to keep away from each other. We are not to communicate or even send a text. But the thing is, Kale has already tried to contact me."

"Why, if he knows not to?" the priest asked.

"Because I think he is missing me as much as I'm missing him," I sighed. "But I can't risk getting into any more trouble at work for fear of being kicked off the force."

"So there is your dilemma," the priest sighed. "I understand now. Let down your friend or risk losing your job."

"Correct," I said. "Both are really important to me."

There was another pause, then Father Rochford said, "If you don't mind me asking, what sort of trouble have you and Kale got into?"

"We both love solving mysteries, that's why we both joined the police force," I said. "We love figuring things out and I think we're both good at it. But our sergeant thinks we're starting to run before we've learnt to walk. I guess he only has our best interests at heart."

"Sounds like you came out here to run away," the priest said.

"Run away from what?" I said, scraping a loose strand of hair behind my ear.

"From making a decision," he smiled knowingly.

"How come?" I asked, although in my heart I knew what he meant.

"All the way out here so your friend Kale can't reach you I bet?" the priest said. "I bet you have your phone switched off. I bet you haven't told your friend or anyone else where you are. So when you get back you can say to Kale that you didn't return his calls because you came away to visit your father's grave and there was no signal in such a remote place..."

"You see a lot," I smiled, feeling a little embarrassed. Was I so easy to read?

"Am I right?" he smiled.

"Spot on," I said. "I'm going to stay at The Hook Inn a few miles from here. "You're right, I want to be unreachable for the next few days. I knew that if I stayed back in Bleakfield, I'd be tempted to go and see my friend."

"Are you sure he is *just* a friend?" Father Rochford gently probed. "You sound as if you think a lot of Kale."

"He's just my friend," I said. "In fact, I've never had a boyfriend."

"Never?" the priest asked looking surprised.

"Never."

"Well should you change your mind, Kale, will be a very lucky man indeed. You seem to have a very kind heart and a warm smile, November Lake," he said.

"Thank you," I said, feeling my cheeks glowing hot and it wasn't from the warmth of the autumn sun I could feel.

There was another pause, and I sat and watched the leaves blowing about the gravestones. I felt better for talking to the kind priest, and I was just about to tell him that I thought I should be heading off, when he started up the conversation again.

"November, you said you like solving mysteries."

"Yes," I nodded.

"Perhaps then you could help me solve one," he said, and for the first time since meeting him, that glint in his eyes had faded.

"What's the mystery?" I asked, my interest already growing deep inside of me.

Father Rochford looked at me, his smile gone and now replaced with a look of dread. "To my horror, every morning when I wake up, I discover that someone has crept into my house and left a butcher's knife lying on the carpet outside my bedroom door," he said.

Kale

Perhaps the problem was you never truly realised what you had until it was taken away from you. But why did I feel as if I had lost something so important now? It was like a hole had appeared in my day somehow and I just didn't know what to fill it with. I couldn't spend my day kicking my heels. Surely I could find something to do. Christ, I was bored on day one, how would I feel during the rest of the week? Perhaps a zombie massacre would pass the time. I switched on my PlayStation again. But I was being shot to ribbons by the horde of zombies staggering across the TV screen. I didn't really have my eye on the game as I kept checking my phone positioned on the sofa beside me.

Perhaps the phone was broken. It was old and on one of those pay-as-you-go deals. I'd had problems with it for months. Pausing the game, I picked up the phone and shook it like a rattle. I looked down at it. Still no message from November. I shook it again until my arm started to ache, then had a thought. Perhaps the message I had sent the previous day to November hadn't been sent. The phone was so bloody old that perhaps the message had been trapped in the ether somewhere. Maybe it was floating around in one of those clouds that people spoke about but never truly understood myself. The only cloud I knew was the one my own freaking head was stuck in.

Leave November alone, I told myself, tossing the phone aside.

But I couldn't. I missed her company. It was as simple as that. And I was bored. I picked up the phone again and sent the following text:

Hey November, r u there?

I got up from the sofa and went and stood by the window, holding the phone aloft in my fist as if it would somehow help send the message through the ether – the clouds. I looked down at the illuminated screen. Message sent, the words on it read.

"Okay," I said, heading toward the kitchen, the phone still clutched in my hand.

I searched through the cupboards for anything that resembled food. Perhaps I should go to the supermarket and…

Are you kidding me? I told myself and reached in for the Pot Noodle that sat at the back on the cupboard. I switched on the kettle and waited for it to boil. It seemed to take forever. I was sure that it didn't usually take this long.

I guess it did when I was bored out of my mind. Everything seemed to be moving slower – taking longer – today. Each second seemed like a minute, each minute like ten, each hour an eternity. I splashed hot water onto the noodles and stuffed a fork into the pot. I went back to the window and watched the rain as I ate the noodles.

November

Now how could I ignore a statement like that? "What did you say?" I asked Father Rochford, just in case I had misheard him the first time.

He pushed his glasses up onto the bridge of his nose. "For the last week, when I wake in the morning, I open my bedroom door to find that someone has left a butcher's knife on the floor."

"Besides you, who else lives in the house?" was my first question, my mind already setting about solving the mystery. It was like I couldn't help myself.

"No one," the priest said, getting up from the bench. "Come with me and I'll show you."

I followed the priest amongst the headstones and across the graveyard. The sun had disappeared behind the clouds, taking its warmth with it. I pulled my coat tightly about me. Father Rochford led me around the side of the dilapidated church and toward a house tucked away from behind a crop of trees. If it had been summer or spring, and the branches had been bristling with leaves, then the house would have been hidden from view. The house was large and sprawling, made from a black Devonshire slate. It looked to be hundreds of years old. Ivy crawled over the front and had been cut back in places to reveal the lower and upper windows. Some of these had been boarded over with planks of wood. There was a brown front door with an iron knocker fixed in to it. Just like the church, one side of the house had scaffolding supporting it. The slate roof appeared intact, but one of the two chimneys looked like nothing more than a pile of rubble. I could see that someone had once gone to the trouble of planting some flowerbeds at the front of the house, but they had long since been neglected and were now just a mountain of thorny-looking bushes. A crow flapped out of the nearby trees and landed on the roof. It angled its head as if watching us with his beady black eyes. As we drew closer to the house, it released an ear-splitting squawk, then, flapping its black feathered wings, it flew back towards the trees.

"So you live here all alone?" I asked, staring up at the house.

"For the last couple of weeks I have," he said. "The church and the house are going to be sold off."

"Why?" I asked.

"The congregation has fallen so low in number over the years, that it's practically non-existent," the priest said regretfully. "As you can see, the church and the house both need extensive repairs, but what is the point if no one ever comes to worship? The parish can't afford to waste what little money it does have. In the past, funds would have been raised by holding summer fetes, raffles, and collections, but with no congregation it is impossible to raise the money to make the repairs. I have been sent to oversee the sale of the house and the grounds. No doubt some developer will snap it up and build apartments or an out of town shopping mall. To be honest, I no longer care. I just want to leave this place. I get the feeling that for whatever reason, I'm not wanted here."

"Why about the graveyard?" I asked. "My father is buried here."

"The graveyard will be left alone," he said.

"Is that why you think a knife is being placed outside your bedroom door each night?" I asked him. "To scare you away?"

"Yes," he said.

I looked back at the house, the wind blowing harder now and making the barren and twisted branches creak overhead. My long hair blew across my face, and I clawed it away. "So someone is breaking in at night, is that what you think?"

"If they are, then I don't know how," Father Rochford said. "There is never any sign of a break-in. I know the house looks as if it needs work, but it is secure."

"No broken windows, doors, or locks?" I asked him.

"None," he said, staring at the house.

"Who else would have keys?" I said.

"There was once a housekeeper, but she died three years ago and was never replaced," Father Rochford explained. "There was a gardener, too, but he would never have been given a set of keys. Anyway, he left soon after the housekeeper passed."

That explained the overgrown flowerbeds, I thought. "Perhaps someone has the keys which once belonged to the housekeeper?" I asked, considering all possible options.

"When Father Boyed left last year, the house was going to stand empty, so new locks were fitted. I have the only set of keys," he said, taking them from his trouser pocket and showing them to me.

"Have you contacted the police?" I said.

"And report what?" he shrugged. "Nothing has been stolen and there has been no break-in."

I looked back at the house. "If no one is breaking in and you have the only set of keys, then that only leaves one option," I said.

"And what is that?" he asked.

"Whoever is leaving the knives outside your bedroom door is also living in the house," I said.

"But that is impossible," the priest gasped. "I am the only one living there."

"Are you sure about that?" I said, heading up the overgrown path toward the house.

I stood at the front door and Father Rochford joined me. "I think you're mistaken," he said, sliding the key he held in his hand into the lock and pushing the door open.

Stepping inside, I was met at once by a waft of musty damp air. I was standing in a large hallway. There was a closed door on either side of me, and ahead there was a wide staircase, branching away in opposite directions at the top. There was a passageway behind the stairs that led deeper into the vast house.

"Do you mind if I take a look around?" I asked the priest.

"Not at all," he smiled. "However, you won't find anyone living here other than me."

I approached the closed door to my right and gripped the cold brass door handle. I turned it and pushed. The door was stiff and creaked open on a set of unoiled hinges. The room I looked into was in darkness, the wooden boards I had seen from outside, covering the windows. I felt along the wall with my hand, my fingertips brushing over the light switch. I flipped it on. The room stayed in darkness.

"I'm afraid the electrics are a bit hit and miss," the priest said over my shoulder. "It's the damp, I think. Got into the circuits."

I closed the door, crossed the hall, and pushed open the opposite facing door. The overcast light from outside seeped through the curtained windows. Dust motes floated in the shafts of pale light. Wooden crates were stacked almost to the ceiling.

"As you can see, I spend most of my days packing so the house can finally be cleared next week," Father Rochford said, coming to stand beside me in the open doorway. "That's what I don't understand."

"What's that?" I asked him.

"As you can see, there is nothing of any great value here," he said, looking at the boxes he had packed and stacked ready for removal. "Why would anyone want to scare me away from here? There is nothing of any value to be had."

"One man's junk is another's treasure," I said, stepping out of the room and back into the hallway.

The priest closed the door and looked at me.

"Can I see where exactly the knife gets left each night?" I asked him.

"Certainly. Follow me," he said, heading across the large open hall toward the stairs.

I followed him upwards onto a small landing where the stairs branched away to the left and right. Darkness lingered like a thick cloud in both directions. The priest headed into the corridor on the right. There was a light switch on the wall and he pressed it with his thumb. A bulb flickered to life overhead, casting the corridor with a dull glow. There were three doors leading off the corridor. As we passed the first, I opened it and looked in at the bathroom on the other side. I closed the door and opened the second. A small bedroom. There was a narrow bed shoved against the far wall, and opposite this was an empty bookshelf. The walls were bare and I could see dark outlines where paintings had once been hung. I closed the door. Father Rochford was waiting for me outside the third doorway, further along the corridor.

"Right here," he said, pointing down at the floor as I joined him. "That's where I find the knife each morning."

I knelt down and inspected the floor, brushing my hand gently over the threadbare carpet. There was nothing to see.

"And this is your room?" I said, getting up and pointing at the door.

Father Rochford pushed open the door. "This is where I sleep."

I looked into the meagre room. It was as bare as the others I had seen. There were no great comforts or luxuries. Just a simple wooden-framed bed, a wardrobe to hang his priestly attire, and a desk and chair by the window.

I stepped into the room, but before I had gone too far, Father Rochford said, "I lock this every night."

I turned to see him pointing to a bolt fitted to the back of the door.

"Do you never venture out of your room once you have locked the door at night?" I asked him.

"No," he said with a shake of his head. "I'm embarrassed to say that I'm a coward. I have lain awake at night listening for any sound, so as to hear this person who leaves a knife outside my room each night, but I don't hear so much as a whisper. But each morning when I open the door, there lays a knife." He pointed to the spot on the floor again.

"Have you got these knives?" I asked him, hoping they might offer up some clue.

"I've thrown them away," he said. "In fact, I've rid the whole house of knives, scissors, or razors. I have kept only one rather blunt butter knife, which I use to eat with."

"What about the knife you discovered this morning?" I asked him. "Have you thrown that away already?"

"No," he said, as if remembering it for the first time. "I have it right here." He went to the desk by the window and pulled open a drawer. He reached inside and took out a long gleaming knife with a serrated edge. It was about thirteen inches long with a razor-sharp blade and wooden handle.

I took the knife from him, turning it over in my hands as I inspected it. The knife looked new. There were no signs of blood or anything else on the blade. The wooden handle was as

41

smooth as glass and without any blemishes of any kind.

The priest held out his hand and I gave it to him. He looked at me as if he were going to say something, but then thought better of it.

"What were you going to say?" I asked him.

He looked at me. "You're a police officer, right?"

"Right," I nodded.

"Would you be interested in staying here tonight and keep watch outside my room for whomever it is leaving these knives?" he asked. "It would be like...what do the police call it? A stakeout."

My first instinct was to say, no. Not because I didn't want to help him, but because I'd been warned by Black not to get involved with any type of crime solving until I returned to training school next week. But my investigative instincts burnt brightly deep within me. The urge to stay the night and discover the identity of the person leaving the knives and their reason why was overwhelming. Despite the knives, I doubted that whoever was leaving them was dangerous. If they were, they would have harmed the priest already. The lock on his bedroom door wasn't the most robust I had even seen and could be broken with one shoulder barge. I suspected that it was a tramp leaving the knives to scare the priest away. They had squatted in the house as it stood empty over the last year. It had become a home to this tramp and he didn't want to be evicted. The knife I had seen was new, and therefore, had probably been stolen by the tramp from a store in the town of Port Haven. Despite the fact the priest believed his temporary home to be secure, I suspected the tramp had discovered a way in and out of the house undetected.

"Please," the priest said, clasping his hands as if he just might drop to his knees at any moment and start praying. "I haven't really slept in a week and to know that you were keeping vigil outside my door would give me great peace of mind."

It would be a simple case to solve, and I had nothing else planned other than some shopping and revision. I would save money by not having to book into The Hook Inn for the night. But what about Black? How would he ever find out? I'd warn the tramp off tomorrow and that would be the end of the matter. Black would never know. What of my friend Kale? He would love to be a part of this adventure. But I couldn't call him even if I wanted to. My phone was buried in the bottom of my overnight bag which was tucked into the top box on the back of my motorbike.

"I'll cook dinner," the priest said, as if to tempt me. "It's getting late already, and by the time you reach Havens Port, the inn there might be fully booked and…"

"Okay, I'll stay and keep watch for you," I sighed with a shrug of my shoulders.

"Thank you, thank you," Father Rochford said, gripping my hands with one of his. He held the knife with the other.

I looked at it gleaming in his fist. "I'd put that away if I were you, before someone gets hurt," I said.

Kale

Come 9 p.m. and still no reply from my friend, November. I knew in my heart Sergeant Black had scared her enough not to respond to my messages. And I liked November enough not to want to get her into trouble. So, switching off my phone, I went to bed.

November

While Father Rochford heated some pizza and garlic bread in the oven, he took me for a tour around the rest of the house. In the rooms where the windows hadn't been boarded over, we double checked to make sure that in fact each of them was locked and secured. With the theory that perhaps the person leaving the knives was holed up in the house somewhere, we went from room to room, checking every corner and checking under and behind any pieces of furniture that hadn't yet been packed away.

"Does the house have an attic?" I asked the priest.

He nodded. "And a cellar, if you want to check them out?"

"I think we should, just to make sure," I said.

We searched the attic first, climbing a set of narrow stairs that wound upwards into the roof. With a simple swipe of a flashlight that Father Rochford had given me, I could see the attic was empty. We made our way down to the cellar. The steps were hidden behind a heavy wooden door. This was padlocked. Father Rochford produced a key from his pocket and unfastened it. Waving the torchlight from side to side, I made my way down into the darkness, the priest at my heels.

"I'm afraid, the lighting doesn't work down here," he said. "It's the dampest part of the house."

I shone the torch into each corner of the cellar and could see nothing of interest. I did notice a small grate in the wall. I walked slowly across the cellar, my footfalls echoing off the stone floor. Standing on tiptoe, I peered through small iron bars. I could see the star-shot sky and the crescent moon in the now dark sky.

"I think the dinner will be ready by now," Father Rochford said. "I'm starving."

Looking back over my shoulder, I watched him heading back up the wooden stairs and out of the cellar. I followed. At the top he closed the door again. In the kitchen I sat at the table as Father Rochford took the pizza from the oven and cut it into thin slices with the butter knife.

"I'm sorry I can only offer you pizza," he said, putting the food on the table before me. "I really hadn't been expecting any visitors."

"Pizza is just fine," I said, picking up a slice.

We sat and talked as we ate. Father Rochford asked why I had wanted to join the police force so young. I explained about my father's murder. He asked if I had any brothers or sisters and I said that I had no family now that my father had died. He asked me why I had been named November as it was kind of unusual and he'd never met someone with the name before.

"My mother liked the name," I shrugged. "That's what my father told me. My mother died when I was very young. I don't really remember her. People call their daughters, May, June and April, so why not November? My mother thought it was pretty, that's all."

I didn't want to talk about my name, it was the first thing that most people asked about when first meeting me. To talk about my mother opened up too many wounds and I had enough of them. So wanting to change the subject, I asked Father Rochford about the history of the house. He explained that from what he understood the house had once been used in the past as a hospital to nurse the sick that were dying from leprosy. At night, nuns would stand outside in the darkness ringing a bell to ward away passing travellers. The house was later used as a manor by a wealthy aristocrat who had servants and maids.

After he had finished talking, Father Rochford looked at his watch. "Where has the time slipped away to?" he said, getting up from the table. I glanced at my own wristwatch and could see that it had just gone 11 p.m. Pushing my chair back from the table, I stood up. There was a short and uncomfortable silence as the priest looked at me.

"November, I appreciate you offering to stay the night but I'm beginning to wonder if you wouldn't be safer if you just left. I should have never put you in this situation. I've been selfish."

"I want to stay and discover who has been trying to scare you," I assured him. "Besides, if I left now, where would I go? Where would I stay?"

"But aren't you scared?" he asked me.

"Cops aren't meant to get scared," I smiled at him, although I could feel a slight flutter in my stomach."

"If you're sure…"

"I'm sure," I said, scooping up the torch from off the table. "Shall we go up?"

Without saying another word, Father Rochford turned out the kitchen light and I followed him through the house and up to his room. Reaching the door, he pushed it open and stepped inside. Before closing it, he looked back at me and said, "Are you sure you will be quite safe?"

"Don't concern yourself about me, father," I said. "Try and get some sleep."

Father Rochford closed the door and I heard the bolt slide into place on the other side of it. I switched off the torch, throwing the corridor into darkness and began my wait.

The longer I waited, the colder I became. A chill draught blew up from the stairs and along the corridor. At just past 1 a.m., I slid down the wall, wrapping my arms around me in an attempt to keep warm. The sense of loneliness washed over me again as I sat alone in the darkness. Instinctively, I reached into my jeans pocket for my phone and then remembered that it was still in the box fixed to the back of my motorbike. And I knew then, that if I had it in my hand I would have responded to the text Kale had sent me. The priest had been right; I had run away so I didn't have to make a decision. However much I didn't want to be thrown out of training school, I didn't want to lose my friend either. We shared instincts and a friendship that was yet to be defined. But one thing I could be sure of was that Kale understood me better than anyone else. I had been able to share my secrets and my feelings about my parents with Kale.

Sergeant Black might have believed he was doing the right thing trying to keep me and Kale apart, but I couldn't accept that. He might be my sergeant and therefore, giving me orders, but he had no right telling Kale and me to keep a part. He didn't have the right to choose my friends for me. It was my right to do that and I was taking that back with or without Black's permission. The first thing I would do tomorrow morning, after I'd unmasked the person leaving the knives, would be to call Kale up and see if he wanted to join me in Port Haven for the next few days…

A sudden noise came from downstairs. I sprang to my feet. It came again. Like someone was shuffling around below. With the torch still off and my heart now thumping, I crept along the corridor to the small landing at the top of the stairs. I peered over the banister, and although I could hear someone moving around down in the darkness below, I couldn't see them. I switched on the torch. A fleeting shadow raced away beneath the stairs and back toward the kitchen.

I pressed the light switch at the top of the stairs, the same one I had seen Father Rochford use early that evening. But this time the light didn't flicker on. So, with my only source of illumination the cone of light shining from the end of my torch, I raced down the stairs after the fleeting shadow. I heard the sound of movement in the darkness ahead of me and I aimed the torch in that direction. The outline of a figure raced away around the bend in the passageway and headed in the direction of the kitchen. I chased after it, my heart beating in my chest and ears. I rounded the corner and headed for the kitchen. The door was open. I drew to halt, my chest hitching up and down as I drew breath. Peering ahead, I listened for any sound of movement. There was only silence. I crept forward, hand gripped around the handle of the torch in case I had to use it as a weapon to defend myself. Reaching the kitchen, I tiptoed around the doorway, shinning the torch beneath the table, then into the corners. The kitchen was empty. So where had the figure gone? I inched my way toward the windows. All of them were securely locked from the inside, as was the backdoor.

A sudden noise came from above. I instinctively shone the torch upwards, illuminating the cracked ceiling. More movement above me. Spinning around, I raced back across the kitchen, down the passageway, and to the foot of the staircase. I climbed them, two at a time, until I reached the top. How had the person managed to slip past me? Had they been hiding in the shadows somewhere and stepped out as I had raced past in search of them? I headed down the corridor and back toward Father Rochford's room. It was then I saw it, gleaming back at me, reflecting off the torchlight. I reached down and picked up the knife that now lay on the floor outside the priest's bedroom door. I shone light over it and could see that it was identical to the one I had seen earlier.

I heard the bolt on Father Rochford's bedroom door rattle. The door opened, and he peered bleary-eyed through the gap he had made.

"November?" he said. Then, noticing the knife in my hand, he added, "Where did you get that?"

"I found it outside your door," I told him.

He opened the door wider and peered along the corridor. His hair stuck out from either side of his head as if he had just woken. "You have the culprit then?"

"No," I said with a shake of my head.

"Then how...?" he frowned, looking down at the knife, then back at me. "How did you get that knife?"

"I'm not sure, exactly," I breathed, looking at the knife I held in my hand. "But whoever left it here I think has gone now."

"How can you be so sure?" he asked, daring to poke his head around the doorframe again and peer along the corridor and into the gloom.

"Because they've done what they came to do," I said, holding out the knife. "There is nothing more I can do tonight."

"Perhaps you're right," he said. "You look tired."

"I am," I told him.

"Go and get some rest in the spare bedroom," he said, pointing down the corridor.

"I think I will," I said, taking the knife with me.

As I stood outside the bedroom door, I heard Father Rochford step back into his room and throw the bolt. I stepped into the spare room and locked the door behind me. I stood with my back pressed flat against it, heart racing and looked down at the knife. I knew who had left it outside in the corridor. Father Rochford.

I shone the torchlight onto the hilt of the knife and looked at my initials, *NL,* which I had scratched earlier into the wood with my thumbnail. I had then handed the knife back to the priest, warning him to put it away before someone got hurt. I'd then watched him lock it back in the desk drawer in his bedroom before leading me downstairs for dinner. Father Rochford had been the only person to have access to that knife. So while I had been chasing shadows in the dark downstairs tonight, he had crept from his room, placing the knife on the floor outside his room.

But why? And who had it been I had seen in the dark below? Were there two people living in the house, like I had first suspected? Had one distracted me, while Father Rochford had positioned the knife? If so, why? The mystery I had come across was far deeper and darker than I had first believed. All I could do was wait until morning before I made my next move.

Sitting on the edge of the bed, I stared out of the window and toward the graveyard where my father lay. I was too scared to sleep.

Kale

I woke early. My sleep had been restless. An uneasiness had penetrated my sleep and left me with a feeling that November might be in some kind of trouble. As I got out of bed and padded to the bathroom, I checked my feelings to make sure I wasn't conjuring up excuses just so I could disobey my sergeant and contact her. But it felt much more than that. After showering and putting on some clean clothes, I switched my brick back on and checked for messages. There weren't any. With the sense of unease still nagging away at the back of my mind, I called

November. I paced my room again. There was no ringing tone and my call went straight to voicemail. November had her phone switched off. "Hey, this is November Lake," her recorded message started. "I can't come to the phone right now. But leave your name and number and I'll call you right back." There was an ear-piercing bleep, urging me to leave a message.

"November, it's Kale. I know we've been told to keep apart this week, but this problem – mystery – has come up. It's the strangest thing I've ever come across and it would be great to have your help – you know, me and you working together. I can understand if you don't want to, but at least give me a call." I paused, then taking a deep breath and not wanting to deceive my friend, I added, "Look, the whole thing about the mystery is a lie. Just give me a call. I won't answer so technically we haven't spoken, but just let me know you're okay. Okay? If you don't call my phone within the next hour then I'm going to come over and we will both be in the shit with Black." I ended the call and looked at my watch. It was 7 a.m.

At just past 8 a.m., I threw on my coat, got in my car, and headed for November's house. I pulled up outside, and the first thing I noticed was that the sleek black motorbike she rode was missing. Had it been outside yesterday during my drive-by? I closed my eyes as I tried to remember. I couldn't be sure that it had been. Climbing from my car, I went to the front door. I rapped against it with my knuckles. There was no answer – not even a sound from within. I stepped back from the door and onto the pavement. I glanced up at the window where she liked to sit. November wasn't there. But then again, why would she be if her motorbike was missing? She was out. But where, and why so early?

What's it got to do with you? I told myself, heading back to my car.

I stopped and looked back up at her window. The curtains were pulled shut. Had they been like that yesterday? I closed my eyes. Yes, they had. Where could she be? She didn't have any family she could visit. Maybe she had gone to stay with a friend. But November was like me, she didn't really have friends, just acquaintances, and you never went and stayed with them.

I leant against my car, arms folded across my chest, and stared up at November's window. I thought of all those piles of newspapers in her poky flat. Perhaps she had discovered some clue – a piece of information – relating to her own father's death. But why have her phone switched off for the last couple of days? That nagging feeling told me there was something more to this than November not wanting to take calls or messages from me. Stepping away from my car, I went to her front door again. I pushed against it with my fingertips. It was shut tight. I looked back over my shoulder, then left and right up the street. There was no one about. Taking a step back, I drove my shoulder against the front door. It rattled in its frame. I hit the door again, this time harder. It creaked. I forced my shoulder against it, and this time the door popped open. I slipped inside, closing the door behind me. At the top of the stairs, I tapped on the door, pressing my ear flat against it. I could hear no movement on the other side.

I forced the door like I had the other, until the catch was suddenly sprung.

"Hey, November," I called out, poking my nose around the edge of the door and peering into her flat. "Are you there?"

No answer.

I stepped inside, closing the door behind me. Apart from the piles of old newspapers stacked in one corner, the room was tidy. It didn't look as if there had been any kind of struggle…

"Struggle!" I breathed out loud, fearing that perhaps my imagination was now running away with me. Perhaps I should go? What would happen if November came home and discovered I had broken into her flat? What would I say? That I had an irrational fear something bad had happened to her? That I never really knew how lonely I was until we had been forced apart? That I couldn't stop thinking about her? That I missed her? She might think that I was some kind of stalker – or worse, a pervert.

I looked down at the chair where she sat for hours listening to tunes on her iPod, watching people go about their business below. I ran my fingertips over the back of it, then let them slide away. I should leave. I had broken into my friend's flat – her home – and invaded her privacy. I stepped away and it was then I noticed the note on the coffee table. Reaching down, I picked it up and read the list that November had scribbled across it.

Visit Dad's grave at the Sacred Heart.
Stay at the Hook Inn
Go shopping
Revise for police exam
Keep away from Kale (although I don't really want to!).

I read the last line, a grin spreading across my face. So it did seem that November had gone away. It looked like she was going to visit her father's grave, do some shopping, revise for her police exam, and keep away from me. But the note said that she didn't really want to. Why then not answer my texts or at least call my phone to let me know she was okay?

"Just leave her in peace," I said, trying to talk over that nagging feeling that just wouldn't go away.

If I wasn't careful, November wouldn't want to be my friend. Breaking into her flat was going to be hard enough to explain. Wasn't she entitled to go away for a break without me hounding her? I placed the note back onto the coffee table and left her room, making sure the door was locked behind me. I sat in my car and it started to rain. I fired up the engine, then almost at once switched it off again. The nagging voice whispering in my ear that November was in some kind of trouble just wouldn't go away. Taking my phone out, I dialled Directory Enquires.

A woman answered at once. "What name, please?"

"The Hook Inn," I said.

"In what town, please?"

I didn't know the answer to that question. "The nearest to Bleakfield, please."

There was a pause. "I have a Hook Inn in the town of Port Haven, which is twenty miles…"

"That will be the one," I said.

"Would you like me to text you the number?"

"Yes, please," I said and ended the call.

Within moments, the number had flashed up on the screen of my mobile. I wasted no time in calling it.

"Hook Inn," a man said after three rings.

"I believe you have a guest staying with you called November Lake," I said. "Would you be able to pass a message for me…?"

"November who?" the man grunted down the line.

"Lake. November Lake," I told him again. I could hear the sound of pages being turned in what I guessed was the guestbook.

"Sorry, but we don't have anyone staying here with that name," the man came back.

"Are you sure?" I frowned.

"Wanna come down here and check the register yourself?" he grunted again.

"I just might," I shot back, now sounding as grumpy as he did.

"Goodbye…"

"Please, wait," I said, before he'd had the chance to hang up on me.

"What do you want now?" the man sighed as if he had a million better things to do than talk to me.

"Give me a break," I said, hoping that I didn't sound too needy. "I'm just trying to find my friend that's all. It's almost like she has disappeared. She is eighteen, has long straight blonde hair, and really pretty. You would remember her if you saw…"

"Got no one staying here like that," the man cut in. "If that's all…"

"No, wait," I said. "Could you give her a message from me just in case she does arrive?"

"Don't you kids text each other these days?" the man sighed again.

"She's not answering her phone…" I started.

"Had a lover's quarrel, have you?" the man chuckled. The thought of such a thing obviously brightened his mood.

"No, nothing like that," I shot back. "Tell her to ignore what Black said and give me a call. I just want to know she is okay."

"Who's Black?" the man asked. "He's not the boyfriend, is he? I don't want any trouble…"

"There won't be any trouble," I tried to assure him.

"There had better not be," he warned. "Now if that's all, I've got work to…"

Then thinking of the note November had left behind, I cut in and said, "Is there a church close by to you call the Sacred Heart?"

"On the outskirts of town," he said. "But if you're thinking of trying to persuade this November girl to walk up the aisle with you, then forget it. It ain't no proper church anymore."

"What do you mean?" I asked.

"The place has been taken over by one of those crazy religious sects," he said, his voice now dropping to a whisper as if passing on some salacious gossip.

"What do you mean, a religious sect?" I pushed. "November's father was buried there a few years ago."

"The priest must have left soon after, because the church and the house have been sold," the man explained. "We were all sad to see it go, but people had just stopped worshipping there, and I heard the cost of the repairs was too much…"

"What about this sect?" I reminded him.

"Some guy calling himself Father Rochford bought the place just a few weeks ago," he said, his voice still just a whisper. "But I've heard rumours that he's not like a real priest. He runs some kind of cult… but you know what gossip can be like… he's probably a decent chap…"

"What's the address of this church?" I snapped.

The man told me and I wrote it down on a cheeseburger wrapper I found in the glove box.

"Thank you," I said, and ended the call. Tossing my phone onto the passage seat, I started up the car and headed for the outskirts of Port Haven.

November

I sat by the window all night. I didn't move. At dawn, I heard Father Rochford leave his room and walk down the corridor. He stopped outside my door. I sat on the end of the bed and watched his shadow beneath the door. He was out there several minutes, before moving slowly off again. From below, I heard the front door swing open then closed. As quietly as I could, I got up from the bed, and lingered by the window. I watched Father Rochford head away from the house, past the overgrown flowerbeds and toward the church. As he reached the cluster of trees on the edge of the graveyard, he suddenly turned around and stared up at the window where I watched him from. I gasped, dropping back down onto the bed.

Had he seen me? I couldn't be sure.

I counted my heartbeats until my breathing had slowed. Very carefully, I peered out of the window again. To my relief I could just see Father Rochford, dressed all in black, head around the side of the rickety church and disappear from view. As I'd sat through the night at the window, I struggled to find a reason why Father Rochford would have wanted to place the knife on the floor outside his own room. Perhaps he was worried that I hadn't believed his story, and if he laid the knife on the floor I would be convinced to stay and keep guard until he left the house at the end of the week? Perhaps he had been scared so much, that he had become desperate and lost all reason. But there had been something else, too, that I couldn't quite get from my mind. As I had gone into his room the previous day, he had called me back to inspect the lock. Had he really wanted me to see the lock? It was just like any other. Had there perhaps been something in the room he feared I might *see*? And that's what I needed to find out. If there was something that he was trying to hide, it might be the answer to solving the mystery of Father Rochford.

I looked out of the window one last time to make sure he wasn't heading back toward the house. Unable to see him walking along the overgrown path outside, I slid back the bolt on my door and crept from my room. Very little natural light shone into the corridor, so with the torch in one hand and the knife in the other, I made my way toward Father Rochford's bedroom. Standing outside it, I glanced back down the corridor to make sure that I was alone. Seeing nobody there, I switched off the torch and placed it in my trouser pocket. I then turned the handle and slipped into the bedroom. Keeping the door ajar, so I could hear if anyone should come down the corridor, I crossed to the middle of the room. What was it he didn't want me to see? I thought, studying the room. There was very little for me to inspect. Then, just when I thought perhaps I had been wrong about the priest trying to hide something from me, I noticed what it might have been. Placing the knife on the desk, I crouched down on the floor by the bottom of the wardrobe. I brushed my fingertips gently over the carpet. Patches of it looked as if it had been worn away. But not because the carpet was old, but because the wardrobe had been repeatedly pulled away from the wall and pushed back into place again.

Standing, I gripped the sides of the wardrobe and heaved it back from the wall. I peered into the gap I had made. There was a small door fixed into the wall, hidden by the wardrobe. Taking a deep breath, I squeezed myself into the gap and pushed the door with my hand. It swung open. I poked my head around the edge of the door, pulling the torch from my pocket. I switched it on and gasped at finding what appeared to be a secret passageway running between the walls of the house. On tiptoe, I stepped inside.

Kale

With the rain and wind lashing against the side of my car, I raced toward the town of Port Haven. The tight country roads were slippery and the back of my car spun out across the road more than once. I gripped the steering wheel and bit my lower lip as I tried to keep control of my car. I knew the general direction I needed to take to get to the town, but the church was on the outskirts and I had no idea exactly where. Why didn't I have one of those smart phones like November? I could use Google maps or whatever it was called to locate the place. I scowled at my brick that lay on the passenger seat beside me.

"You're gonna have to go," I snarled at it.

I looked up to see a bend in the narrow road. I hit the brakes, the rear of my car sliding left then sharply right. I brought the car under control and raced around the bend in the direction of Port Haven. Should I phone Sergeant

Black? Tell him what had happened or what I feared had happened to November?

"Hey, sarge, November has been ignoring my calls, just like you told her to," I said, starting an imaginary conversation with myself. "But my ego became bruised and I couldn't accept that she didn't want to speak to a gorgeous guy like me, so I went and broke into her flat, nosed through her personal notes, discovered that she had gone away to visit her father's grave and revise for her police exams. So, for no real good reason other than it was easier for me to believe that she had come to some harm instead of simply not wanting to speak to me, I telephoned the inn where she was staying. The innkeeper told me that he had never heard of her, but there was a church not too far away where some dodgy priest had set up some cranky church for him and his fellow occultists. My copper's nose was now telling me that November was going to be used as a human sacrifice."

I cringed at how that sounded. It was ridiculous and paranoid. If I repeated any of that to Sergeant Black I wouldn't only be off the force but be sitting in a white padded cell somewhere. No, I couldn't call him. Not until I had more than my paranoid imagination to go on.

Reaching the outskirts of Port Haven, I slowed the car and meandered around the narrow roads. I peered through the rain-smeared windscreen for any sign of the church. The countryside was barren and featureless, not like the rolling hills of the Peak District where I had been raised by my mother and father. There was a T junction ahead. I slowed the car and looked left then right. It was then, in the distance to my right, I saw the black twisted spire of a church poking up from behind a crop of leafless trees. I headed toward it.

November

The secret passageway was so narrow that my shoulders brushed against the walls on either side of me. I shone the torch up and down and from side to side. I could see that the passageway had been used very recently. If it hadn't, then the place would be infested with spider webs and dust. But there were no webs in the corners and no dust on the floor. I reached the end of the passage and found myself staring down into a deep black stairwell. I glanced back to see the chink of light that seeped from Father Rochford's room around the edge of the wardrobe and into the passage. Looking front again and shining the torchlight into the dark, I headed down the stairs.

At the bottom I found myself in another passageway identical to the one I had left behind. I followed it until I came to another door. I pressed the side of myself against it and trying to keep my racing heart under control, I listened for any noise that might come from the other side. Taking a step back and shining the torchlight against the door, I noticed that there was a hatch at eye height. I pulled it to one side and pressed my eye up against it. The room on the other side was in darkness. There was a bolt at the top of the door, and, sliding it to one side, I pushed the door open. Holding the torch out before me, I stepped into the room, recognising it at once. I was in the cellar. As I looked at the stairs which I had followed the priest up the night before, I realised how he had left the knife outside his own bedroom.

"You've figured it out, haven't you?"

I turned around to find the priest standing in the doorway which led from the secret passage and into the cellar. He no longer wore his priestly clothes, but a long, black flowing robe with a hood that was pulled over his head. The torchlight glinted off the knife he held in his hand.

"Yes," I said, taking a step back toward the stairs.

"If you're thinking of escaping, November, you shouldn't bother," he smiled. "The door at the top of the stairs is locked."

"It wasn't last night though, was it?" I said. "As I sat and kept watch outside your door, you crept from your bedroom via the secret passageway. You came to this room, you climbed the stairs back into the house where you made a noise to draw my attention. Knowing that I would leave my vigil to come and investigate, you waited in the shadows at the bottom of the stairs. Then when I had sight of you, you raced back down into the cellar, through the secret passageway, and back to your room, where you opened the door, positioning the knife on the floor for me to find. You then locked your door again and pretended you had been asleep the whole time. But once I inspected the knife, and the saw the mark I had left earlier, I knew it was you who had repositioned the knife, but what I didn't know was why," I said as he stood blocking my only escape from the cellar.

The priest smiled and it was no longer a friendly look, but sly and sinister. "This is a new kind of church and I'm its leader. My fellow brethren will be joining me here soon."

"Those boxes I saw in the rooms upstairs," I said, "You were unpacking not packing."

He smiled again. "Very good, November Lake. You really do like solving a good mystery, don't you?"

"There never was anyone leaving knives outside your room, was there?" I asked him, but already knowing his reply and understanding how he had trapped me. He had created the mystery to entice me to stay. He knew too that a young, eager cop was even less likely to walk away without helping him. I'd also told him that no one knew where I was.

"No," he grinned beneath his hood. He stepped away from the door, coming closer. "Finding you alone in the graveyard saved me the trouble of enticing a pretty young girl here for me and my brethren to sacrifice in honour of our new church. It was as if it was meant to be – as if it was what God wanted."

I watched as he took a step closer. "Is that how you show your appreciation to God, by destroying his most precious gift, life?" I said, inching back and nearer to the damp, moss-covered wall of the cellar. There was nowhere for me to run.

"God will appreciate the sacrifice of such a pretty and pure life as your own," he reasoned with his own sick and twisted logic. "But first I will make you my bride." He was now within touching distance, and he reached out with one cold hand and caressed my cheek. He moistened his dry-looking lips with the tip of his tongue. "To kill such a beautiful and pure bride before enjoying the flesh will truly be a sacrifice. One of the hardest I have ever had to make. God will appreciate that."

In the gloom of the cellar, I felt the cold steel edge of the blade slide slowly across my throat.

Kale

My heart leapt at the sight of November's motorbike. It was parked beneath a nearby tree at the entrance to a drab-looking graveyard. I stopped my car next to her motorbike and got out. I could see bird droppings over the black bodywork of her bike. I looked up at the tree branches and the blackbirds squawking in them. Some of the droppings were dry and crusty, telling me that November's car had been parked for a day or more. But where was November? Why had she left her car here, and why had she never made it to The Hook Inn?

I looked across the graveyard and could see a dilapidated church. It was in desperate need of repair. Had November decided to take a look around the inside of the church but stumbled across some Black Mass being performed by the cultists the man at The Hook Inn had spoken of? But had that all just been gossip? Did such sects even exist? I weaved my way through the chipped and cracked headstones. Standing in front of the church, I looked up at the spire that reached up into the overcast sky like a broken finger. It looked as if it might collapse at any moment. I pushed against the weather-beaten church door, but it wouldn't budge. There was a big iron handle, which I yanked left and right, but still the door wouldn't open. I stepped back from the door, blowing out my cheeks. I headed around the side of the church. There was a crop of trees, and behind these I could see what looked like a house. Was this where these Satanists live? Who said they were Satanists? Was I letting my imagination run away with me? But I just couldn't shake off that overpowering sense of foreboding I felt in my heart. The graveyard, the church, and now the house I could see between the trees gave off an oppressive feel. Shouldn't a church have a sense of welcoming, peace, and tranquillity? Nothing about this place made me feel easy.

I followed the overgrown path up to the front door. I knocked on it with my knuckles. I waited, but there was no reply. No sound from inside. With my unruly mop of hair blowing back from off my brow, I stepped over the thorny flowerbeds and went to the nearest window. It was boarded over with planks of wood. I tried to prise one of them away from the window so I could take a peek inside. Just like the church door, I couldn't get it to budge, however much I yanked on it. Looking to my right, I could see another window that hadn't been boarded over. I went to it, and cupping my hands around my eyes, I peered in through the dirty windows. Sighing, I stepped backwards. Heavy drapes hung at the windows, blocking my view.

"Give me a break," I sighed out loud. I wouldn't give up.

With hands thrust into my trouser pockets and hunched forward, I made my way around the side of the house. The wind blew all about me, chucking up gusts of dead leaves which fell like burnt confetti. Nearing the back of the old house, I thought I heard voices. I stopped dead in my tracks, cocking my head to one side. Was it just the howl of the wind I could hear? The voices came again. One female, the other male. I was sure if it. But where were they coming from? I moved slowly forward, the voices becoming gradually louder – clearer. Was that November I could hear talking? If so she sounded upset. Scared?

Standing dead still, I tried to block out the sound of the wind and focus on the voices. It was as if they were seeping up from beneath the ground. I crouched low, placing one side of my head against the grass. It was then I saw it. There was a small grate fixed into the wall at the base of the house. I crawled toward it, placing one eye against the mesh. I held my breath as I peered down into what looked like a darkened cellar. November was standing in the murky gloom, the only light coming from the torch she held in her hand. She was talking to someone, and she sounded scared. Careful not to be heard, I repositioned myself and peered down into the darkness. I could just make out what looked like a tall figure wearing a black hooded robe. It was impossible for me to see this person's face, but I knew he was a man, as I could hear his voice. It was then I saw something glinting in the darkness. The hooded man was holding a knife in his fist and it was pointed at November.

"God will appreciate the sacrifice of such a pretty and pure life as your own," I heard the man say with a cruel delight. "But first I will make you my bride."

From my hiding place I watched him close the gap between himself and November. He reached out and touched her face. I saw

November flinch backwards as if repulsed by his touch.

"To kill such a beautiful and pure bride before enjoying the flesh will truly be a sacrifice. One of the hardest I have ever had to make. God will appreciate that," the hooded man said.

"He is a *Satanist!*" I whispered in shock.

I then saw the man raise the knife and run the blade over November's throat.

November

"November!" a voice shouted.

I looked up to see Kale's face pressed against the other side of the grate. I never thought I would be so glad to see anyone before. Father Rochford looked back too, taking the blade from my throat. Raising the torch above my head, I brought it down, striking the priest. I heard a sickening thud, then Father Rochford wail in pain. The torch winked out, flying from my hand. With my hands stretched out before me, I raced in the direction of the door. I felt blindly for it in the dark. My outstretched hands brushed against the wooden doorframe. I lurched forward and into the secret passageway. The sound of running footsteps were close behind me. I wanted to call out to Kale, but I knew that I would only be highlighting my location for the priest in the darkness. I stumbled and tripped forward in the dark, my hands feeling the walls on either side of me. I should have reached the stairs by now that led up to the corridor and back into Father Rochford's bedroom. If only I could get there before he caught me, then I could lock the door, imprisoning him behind the walls. But I couldn't find the stairs in the darkness, and was sure that I should have reached them by now. The sound of the priest's shallow breathing behind me pushed me on deeper into the darkness of the maze of corridors I now found myself in.

Kale

I saw November strike the hooded man with the torch. But she lost her grip on it. The torch went out, disappearing into the darkness. I strained to see into the cellar, but it was so dark down there now, I couldn't see anything at all. I heard the sound of running footsteps but that was it. I gripped the grate with my fingers, but even if I could tear it free, the gap was way too small for me to climb through and down into the cellar. Scrambling to my feet, I raced back to the front of the house. I tried opening the window with the drapes. But it was stuck fast. Turning, I crouched and thrust my hands into the wild overgrowth brimming beneath the windows. I cried out as thorns and barbs tore at my hands, drawing blood. I closed my fist around a large rock and stood up. Blood ran between my fingers. I raised my hand, and as if throwing a cricket ball, I threw the rock at the window. The glass broke into several sharp splinters. Yanking off my coat, I wrapped it around my arm and then broke away the shards of glass sticking out of the window frame like jagged teeth. With a hole big enough for me to climb through, I dropped my coat and levered myself into the room on the other side of the window. There was a tearing sound. I looked back to see that my trousers had become caught on a piece of glass. Trying to free myself, I lost my footing and went sprawling to the floor. My trouser ripped from the ankle and as far up to my knee. I pulled myself up, my right trouser leg flapping around me like a pair of flares.

I turned around to find that I was in a room stacked high with wooden crates and packing boxes. Weaving amongst them, I made my way to the door and pulled it open. I was standing in a large hallway. The front door was to my right, and there was a door directly ahead and a wide staircase to my left. As I stood in the hallway, I heard the sound of running. And just like it had been hard for me to locate the direction of the voices I'd heard outside, the sound of running was now proving just as hard to trace. It sounded like it was surrounding me, coming at me from all angles. Above one minute, below the next, then to my left and right. It was disorientating as I stood and spun around in the hall, desperate to locate exactly where the sound was coming from. I raced forwards to the foot of the stairs. The noise of running was to my right. It sounded like someone was running between the very walls of the house. I pressed my head against the wall and listened. Someone raced past on the other side. I stepped backwards and remembered how my father had once told me that he'd had a client who lived in a huge house in the country. It had been more of a stately home than a house. My father, who had been hired to act as this man's lawyer, had said his client's home was so big there were corridors set between the walls. Hundreds of years ago, the servants had been forced to use these secret passages so they wouldn't be seen by the master of the house or any visitors he might be entertaining. My father had told me no one would ever have known the passages existed, as the doors to them were often hidden behind fireplaces, cupboards, beneath... staircases.

I stared at the staircase and the shadows behind it. Stooping forward, I stepped into the shadows beneath the stairs. Set back against the wall was a door. A cupboard, perhaps? I would never know unless I opened it. Closing my fist around the cold metal doorknob, I pulled it open and found myself staring into a dark secret passageway. Crouching, I stepped into the darkness and headed in the direction of the sound of running.

November

It felt as if I had been blindfolded and was now being chased through a maze with no beginning or end. I collided with walls, spinning around, searching for the next narrow passageway with my hands. All the while I could hear the priest racing after me.

"November," he whispered from the darkness. "There is no need to be scared. You will be rewarded for your making the ultimate sacrifice."

I stumbled forward, my fingertips tracing the line of the walls. I looked for any chink of light to show where a door might lead me to Kale and safety. I tripped and went sprawling forward onto my front. Crawling forward, I felt cold fingers close around my ankle. I was dragged sharply backwards. With a fist gripping my hair, I was yanked to my feet. I cried out. The priest pressed himself against me in the tight confines of the passageway. I thought I might just suffocate. His breath was hot against my face as he brushed his against mine.

"You'll make such a beautiful bride," he teased in my ear. "But God will shower me with his blessings for sacrificing you. That is why you must die."

"Why?" I whispered, trying to break free of him.

"Because I know who you really are. I know who hides behind that mask of beauty you wear," he said, sounding angry now, as if he had been tricked in some way.

"Who am I?" I gasped, fearing that I might just faint as he bore down on me, crushing my chest.

"You are the devil," he whispered in my ear. "You are the Anti-Christ and I will not be tempted by you."

"You're insane," I mumbled, my head beginning to feel light, gasping for breath as he crushed me against the wall. His body felt like a weight and as he smothered me.

"We'll see who is insane when I open you up," he breathed in my face. "I know I will find a monster lurking inside of you."

The world seemed to grow darker, if that were possible, as I slowly began to lose consciousness. Then, in the darkness I saw what looked like a figure standing at the end of the corridor. My long eyelashes flickered. Was someone really there? My chest hitched up and down as I struggled to draw breath. I felt that cold blade against my throat again. With my eyes closing, and the corridor feeling as if it were swallowing me up, I looked into the darkness again. The figure was closer now.

Kale, is that you? I wanted to say, but there was no air left in my lungs to form the words.

The figure came closer still. The priest seemed unaware of his presence. I closed my eyes, feeling as if I were sinking – dying.

"Want to see the devil, Father?" I heard a voice suddenly whisper out of the black.

"No!" I heard the priest scream.

The knife against my neck suddenly vanished and so did the priest. I opened my eyes and stared into the darkness, which filled the narrow passageway. I gulped down large mouthfuls of air and filled my empty lungs. I looked to where I thought I had seen the figure.

But the darkness was impenetrable again. Then, with my head spinning and I collapsed.

Kale

"No!" I heard someone scream. The voice was so shrill and filled with fear that it was impossible to tell if it had come from a male or female. I stopped dead in my tracks, my own heart racing in the darkness.

"November!" I roared, running in the direction of the noise.

As I followed it, the noise became more distant. I collided with walls, nearly tripping twice over my own feet as I tried to navigate the maze of passages in the dark. Then, I did trip over something lying on the floor. I went sprawling onto my face. There was a groan behind me.

"November?" I whispered, fumbling around in the darkness. "Is that you?

The noise came again, it was very close. I reached out and felt something soft, like silk sliding through my fingers. It was long hair. My fingertips brushed over soft skin. Even in the darkness, and using only my fingertips, I could recognise the beautiful shape of November's face.

"November," I whispered, taking her in my arms.

"Kale?" I heard her murmur as if waking from a deep sleep.

"Yes," I said, wrapping my arms around her.

November

Kale led me back through the darkness and out the doorway he had found beneath the staircase. The dim light that poured into the hallway hurt my eyes, and I covered them with my hands. With his arm about my shoulder, Kale led me toward the front door.

"Let's get out of here," he said.

"But the priest? Father Rochford," I said, lowering my arm.

"I think he must have fled," Kale said.

"Fled?" I said, being led outside by Kale. The wind was still blowing hard and it was just as cold. "There was someone in the corridor with us. Whoever it was scared him away, is that what you think?"

"Probably seeing me was what scared him," Kale said, puffing out his chest. "He knew he was trapped when he saw me."

"What did you say to him?" I asked, vaguely remembering that whoever had been in the corridor had said something about the devil to the priest.

"I didn't say anything," Kale said. "The priest had done a runner before I found you."

"So it couldn't have been you who scared him enough to…" I started, my head still feeling light and my legs weak at the knees.

"He must have heard me in the passageway, knew he was cornered and fled out of one of those secret doorways," Kale tried to explain.

"But I'm sure I saw someone. I heard his voice," I said, placing a hand to my head, trying to rid it of the dizziness I still felt.

"Perhaps you have a secret guardian angel watching over you, November," Kale joked, taking me by the hand and leading me away from the house.

"Perhaps," I whispered back.

I sat in the passenger seat of Kale's car. He sat beside me, his hands resting on the steering wheel.

"What do you think we should do now?" I asked him.

"We'll I think you should wait a little while before you ride your motorbike," Kale said. "You don't look too well…"

"I didn't mean that," I said, looking sideways at him. "I mean if that priest did escape then we should tell someone… Sergeant…"

"Don't even go there," Kale cut in with a horrified look on his face. "We're in enough trouble with Black as it is without him finding out about this little mystery."

"But that priest is dangerous," I said. "He would've killed me if…"

"He's run for the hills," Kale said. "He won't come back here. He'll warn his sad little clan too…"

"But…" I started.

"November, if Black finds out what happened here, then we will both be off the training course and out of the force," Kale warned me. "Is that what you want? This is your chance to find out who killed you father and it's my chance to…"

"To do what?" I asked.

"It doesn't matter now," he said. "But what does matter is that we keep this our secret."

"We're police officers, Kale," I sighed. "We're meant to catch men like Rochford and lock them up, not let them escape."

"We won't be police officers for very much longer if Black finds out about this," Kale tried to reason with me. "Look, if it makes you feel any better, we could write an anonymous letter to the local press letting them know what sort of church is being set up here. The press love that sort of thing. Father Rochford will be exposed, but I doubt he will be back."

I turned my head and looked out of the window at the branches sawing overhead. I tried to remember the man I thought I had seen in the passageway. I remembered how Father Rochford had screamed. Deep within me, something said that Father Rochford wouldn't ever be able to hurt anyone ever again.

I stared at Kale. "Why did you come looking for me?"

Kale met my stare. At first he didn't say anything. Then, shrugging his shoulders, he smiled and said, "I was bored that was all."

There was a pause. We sat and listened to the wind and the rush of leaves as they blew amongst the gravestones.

"Fancy a little break at a place called The Hook Inn?" I said, without turning to look at him and staring down at my hands.

"Sure," he said. "I know the manager well."

Without saying another word, I climbed from Kale's car and went to my motorbike. I would follow him to the inn. Climbing on to my bike, I glanced back one last time at my father's grave. I could see the wind had blown that posy of flowers onto my father's grave again.

Pulling on my helmet and lowering the visor, I started the bike and followed Kale, leaving the house with its secret passages and doorways behind me. And I just couldn't help but feel that perhaps I had stumbled across an even greater mystery I had yet to solve.

The Death at Hook Inn

November

    I knew the man had murdered his wife, Melinda Took. But I just couldn't prove it and that drove me half-crazy.

    Kale had followed me in his gleaming new car as I rode my motorbike along the coastal roads toward the village of Port Haven. How he afforded such a car on his police probationer wages, I didn't know. He'd told me that his father was a partner in his own law firm, so perhaps Kale's parents were helping out while he studied to be a police officer. I had no family to help support me through police training college, although I did received a sizeable sum from the police force as my father had been killed on duty. Some of this I had used to buy my motorbike, but the rest I had put away into savings. My father's grave now lay way behind me in the grounds of the Sacred Heart Church. I couldn't shake off the nagging feeling I had that perhaps Kale and I should have called the local police and told them what we had discovered about Father Rochford and what he was planning to do there. But our sergeant, Black, had warned Kale and me to keep apart over the Halloween vacation. In his eyes, we were trouble when together. Sergeant Black had threatened to kick us out of police training college if so much as a text message passed between us during our autumn break. Kale had broken that rule within a few hours of the sergeant's threat being made when he had sent me the first text. My phone had been switched off, but when I turned it on, I found several missed texts from Kale. Even though I knew Black could end both of our careers before they'd even started, I was glad Kale had texted me. If he hadn't, Kale would never have discovered I was being held captive by the creepy priest, Father Rochford. Kale had saved me – or had he? Hadn't I seen another figure in the darkness of those secret passageways hidden between the walls of the priest's house? Wasn't it that figure that had come to my rescue? But I couldn't be sure. The priest had been suffocating me and I had been losing consciousness fast, so perhaps the figure I thought I had seen had just been a figment of my fading imagination. Perhaps it had been Kale who had scared the priest away after all? Whatever the reason Father Rochford had fled, I believed Kale was right when he said the priest wouldn't ever come back. Father Rochford knew I was a police officer and would certainly fear that my colleagues and I would now be hunting him down. He would go into hiding. Perhaps when I had passed out of training school and didn't have Sergeant Black watching my every move, I could go in search of Father Rochford myself and bring him to justice. I couldn't risk my position in the police force until I had found my father's killer. So I had agreed with Kale to let Father Rochford run for now.

We still had five days of our break from college left. I had already decided to leave Bleakfield and my poky flat for a short break. My intention had been to visit my father's grave and put some distance between me and my friend Kale. But once again we had been drawn back together by another mystery. Knowing that we were miles from home and the prying eyes of Sergeant Black, Kale had decided to let me lead him to a small inn in the village of Port Haven, where we would stay for a few days.

I couldn't face being shut away in my rented rooms surrounded by piles of dog-eared newspapers. But it was more than that. I didn't like the feeling of loneliness I now felt. To be alone had never bothered me before. I enjoyed sitting in my favourite chair and staring out of the window, listening to my iPod. Since meeting Kale, whenever he wasn't around, I felt a sense of overwhelming loneliness. I guessed that he felt the same. I could see that by the number of texts he had sent to me since Sergeant Black had done his best to drive a wedge between us. I suspected Kale enjoyed my company as much as I enjoyed his. We had become friends and I'd never had too many of them. I don't know why. I'd never been bullied at school or anything like that. It was just I felt there was something different about me or perhaps it was the other way around. The other people I knew were different to me. I had found comfort as a child solving puzzles, while other children my age had been happy to play in the park. And that's why being alone had never bothered me, I had become used to it – until I had become friends with Kale. Now those feelings of loneliness squeezed my heart with cold fingers until I couldn't bear being alone anymore.

So when Kale suggested he follow me to The Hook Inn on the outskirts of Port Haven, I had been unable to tell him to go back to Bleakfield. I wanted my friend to be with me.

Kale

November raced ahead of me. Her bike purred like a giant black panther. I watched as she tilted left then right, skilfully taking the narrow bends in the road. The ends of her long hair fluttered out from beneath her crash helmet as she sat forward on her bike like she was in some way fused with the machine. She looked good in her short black leather jacket and hip-hugging blue jeans. November had already decided to stay in a place called The Hook Inn, way before I'd shown up at the Sacred Heart Church and rescued her from that Satanist. She hadn't been so sure that it was me who had saved her from becoming a human sacrifice or worse. November had hinted at the possibility that someone else had been present in those secret passageways running between the walls of the priest's house. But I hadn't seen anyone. I had been the only one there. If there had have been someone else I would have seen him. Besides, who else knew we were there? No one. And that's the way we had to keep it. Neither me nor November could risk letting Sergeant Black know that we had disobeyed his orders to stay apart over the Halloween break from police training college.

But why should we stay apart? We were just friends after all. Nothing more. And what if there was more? What if November and I did become more than friends? What did it have to do with Black? We were both adults. If November and I were old enough to be cops, then we were old enough to choose... choose what? Who we were going to date. Who was I kidding? November didn't like me like *that*. But did I really like her like *that?* Was I mixing up the obvious feelings I had of friendship for her with something more? It was exciting to be with November. She was like no other girl I had ever met. There I go again – kidding myself. What other girls? I'd spent my life so far at an exclusive boarding school for boys. I didn't know any other girls other than November. She was my first and only girl*friend*. And I emphasise the friend part of that word.

How was I meant to understand the feelings deep inside of me if I'd never had such feelings before? Perhaps sharing some time with November at the inn in Port Haven might make me see things more clearly. After all, if November could *see* clues a mile away, why couldn't I see what was staring me straight in the face?

November

It was just before dusk when I pulled up outside The Hook Inn. There was a small car park at the front for just a few cars. It was off the beaten track and the surrounding landscape was barren and featureless. As I climbed from my bike and removed my crash helmet, I glanced over the fields which led down to the cliffs and the ocean. I doubted the view looked any less dreary on a bright summer's day. Giant slabs of granite rock protruded from the uneven fields giving the landscape a prehistoric feel.

"Wow," Kale breathed, getting from his car. "What a picturesque place you've found us."

"You can always go back to Bleakfield," I said, hoping that he wouldn't.

"What, and leave you out here all alone?" he said, puffing out his chest in an act of mock bravado. "This place looks like something out of *The Hound of The Baskervilles*."

"Then let's get inside, Watson, before the hounds show up," I said, taking my rucksack from the top box on my bike and heading toward the inn.

"So if I'm Watson, who does that make you? Sherlock-freaking-Holmes? I'm not your sidekick," Kale said, following me. Then looking up at the inn, with its crooked walls, narrow dark windows, and twisted chimney stack, Kale whistled through his teeth, and added, "I've seen this place before, too."

"Where?" I said, stopping and glancing at the inn.

"In that movie an *American Werewolf in London*," he said.

I sighed. "It's nothing like that. I think it looks rather charming."

"Yeah, and you'd probably say the same thing about Dracula's castle," he smiled sideways at me.

"C'mon, Miss Marple," I sighed, elbowing him in the ribs. "Let's book in and get something to eat. I'm starving."

The inn was just as I remembered it to be when I'd stayed on the night before my father's funeral. It hadn't changed. The same faded paintings hung from the stone walls. The ceiling was a criss-cross maze of ancient oak beams. There was a fireplace set into the far wall, and flames licked over a smouldering pile of logs. The heat from it warmed my cold hands and face. A few scattered tables were before the fire. An old man sat at one, and another was occupied by a young couple. They were leaning across the table and holding hands.

Kale brushed past me and went to the bar. The last time I'd stayed at the Hook Inn I had been greeted by a middle-aged woman. A man now stood behind the curved shaped bar, a dishcloth thrown over his shoulder. He was tall, at least six-foot-four, and heavily built. His forearms and hands were huge.

"We would like two single rooms please," Kale asked the man.

He took the dishcloth from over his shoulder, wiped his hands on them, and took a leather-bound ledger from beneath the counter. The man thumbed through it. "You're in luck," the man grunted back at Kale.

I doubted very much he needed to check the register to see if he had any spare rooms. I could remember from my last visit that there were only six bedrooms at the inn.

"Great," Kale said. "We'll take them."

"For how long?" the man asked, eyeing me, then Kale.

"Just the two nights," I smiled.

"Breakfast? Dinner?" the man asked.

"That would be great," Kale said.

"That will be ninety-five pounds," he grunted again. "Eighty if you pay cash."

Kale pulled his wallet from the back pocket of his jeans. He opened it and took a peek inside. "I don't suppose..." he said, looking at me embarrassed.

I remembered him telling me he had maxed out his credit cards and had little money until payday. "It's okay," I said, taking four twenty pound notes from my purse and placing them on the bar.

The man snatched them up, then looking at Kale, he said, "So you found her then?"

"Huh?" Kale frowned.

"Your missing friend?" he said. "It was you who called this morning, wasn't it? I recognise your voice."

"Yes, but..." Kale started to waffle.

"You should have heard him," the innkeeper said, turning to look at me. "Scared half to death that you'd run off with some other guy."

"Now, I never said that," Kale cut in, his cheeks flushing red and unable to look at me.

"Yeah, you did," the man insisted much to Kale's embarrassment. "You said you'd had a lovers quarrel."

"It was *you* who said that," Kale shot back, his face now the colour of a plum. I tried to hide my smile.

"You asked me to give some message about some bloke called Black," the innkeeper continued. "You said it was her ex-boyfriend or summin', and I told you I didn't want any trouble." Then, leaning over the bar and staring at Kale, he grunted, "There isn't going to be any trouble, is there?" This was said more as a warning than a question.

"There won't be any trouble as there isn't any ex-boyfriend," I smiled at the innkeeper. "And me and my friend here are just that... friends."

"See," Kale said, fixing the man with an icy stare. "Just *friends*."

"Whatever," the man shrugged, placing two keys onto the bar. "But you told me she was real pretty and you sounded real panicked about her..."

Kale took his key and before the innkeeper had had a chance to finish he was heading away toward a staircase that spiralled upwards into the darkness.

I took my key. "Thank you."

"You're welcome," he said, wiping the dishcloth over the bar.

I turned away.

Before I had taken two steps after Kale, the man spoke again. "I know one thing for sure."

"And what's that?" I said, glancing back over my shoulder at him.

"That boy has the hots for you real bad," he said.

"How can you tell?"

"By the goddamn soppy look he has on his face every time he looks at you. I'm surprised you can't *see* it yourself, November Lake."

I frowned at him. "How do you know my name?"

"Your friend told me it when he telephoned earlier today," the innkeeper smiled, then turned and went back to cleaning the bar.

The innkeeper might have known my name, but he was wrong about Kale liking me more than just a friend. If Kale did, then just like the innkeeper had said, I would've seen it.

Catching up with Kale, I followed him to the top of the stairs. On the landing and out of earshot of the innkeeper, Kale looked at me and said, "Jerk."

"Thanks," I half smiled.

"I didn't mean you," Kale scowled. "I was talking about the idiot behind the bar."

"He was just winding you up," I said, heading down the landing. "Forget it. I have."

The tag hanging from my key had the number six written on it. My room was the last along the narrow landing. I stopped outside the door. Kale stopped outside number five, slipping his key into the lock. I glanced sideways at him.

"Thanks, Kale," I said before he disappeared inside his room. His cheeks were still flushed red.

"For what?"

"Coming to Port Haven with me," I said. "I didn't want to be alone."

"Me neither," he said, stepping into his room and closing the door behind him.

My room was the exact same one I had stayed in before. Nothing seemed to have changed. There was a bed pushed into one corner, a small desk, and a wardrobe. The lampshade was a dark maroon, and when I flipped on the light switch, the bulb did little to brighten the gloom. There was a small bathroom. I placed my rucksack and crash helmet on the bed and sat down. The last time I had sat here, I had been crying for my father. I'd cried for my mother, too, as I'd wished she had been with me – to comfort me at my loss. But she hadn't been there then and wasn't here now. But this time, the tears were easier to fight back and the sense of isolation I felt was less. That was thanks to Kale.

Stripping off my clothes, I ran a warm shower. I stood beneath the water, eyes closed as my tears were washed away. It was then I realised that Kale had no clean clothes to wear or a wash kit. His trip to Port Haven hadn't been planned like mine had. Stepping from the shower, I towelled myself dry and put on some fresh clothes. With my hair still damp about my shoulders, I left my room and went to Kale's.

Kale

"What an arsehole!" I fumed, pushing my door closed.

What was that guy playing at? Trying to embarrass the hell out of me, that's what he had been trying to do. I never said any of that stuff to him when I telephoned the inn earlier in search of November. Sure, I had been worried about her, but that was because he had gone on about the Satanist who had taken over that church. If I had sounded worried about November, it was because of him.

Cheeky git! I thought, glancing about my room. Although it was small, it looked cosy enough. There was a bed beneath the window on the other side of the room, a wardrobe, desk, and a bathroom. Sliding out of my jacket, I dropped it onto the bed and unbuttoned my shirt. I took it off and went to the bathroom. I had no clean change of clothes or anything else with me. When I'd left my rooms in Bleakfield I hadn't expected not to return for a few days. With my credit cards near meltdown, I had no money to buy a fresh change of clothes from the shops in Port Haven. I lifted my arm and I caught a whiff. Phew! I just hoped November liked the rough and ready type. What was her type? Me? Not stinking the way I did. I leaned over the sink and stared at myself in the mirror. I ran the palm of my hand over my chin. It sounded like I was dragging it over glass paper. A coating of stubble covered the lower half of my face. Not good. I ran my hands through my already messy-looking hair. It didn't look neat on the best of days but now it stuck up like I'd just crawled out of bed. Just my luck. I looked and smelt like a goddamn ape. There was a bar of soap. I took it from the wax paper it had been wrapped in. I placed the plug into the sink and began to fill it with hot water. The least I could do was have a quick wash.

There was a sudden knock at my door. Jumping with surprise and with one hand still on the tap, I yanked it. A torrent of water jetted out, splashing the front of my trousers. Shutting off the tap, I looked down at my groin, which was now soaked.

"Oh, Jesus, it looks like I've wet myself!" I groaned out loud. Whoever was knocking at my door was going to think I'd lost control of my bodily functions. Not good!

"Hey, Kale," November called out from the other side of the door.

November! It would have to be. Just my luck, November would come knocking when I looked like an incontinent orangutan.

"Kale, are you there?" She knocked on my door again.

"Just one moment," I called back, pulling down my trousers.

Stepping out of them, I snatched up a towel and threw it about my waist. I glanced one last time into the mirror again, running my fingers through my skewwhiff hair. Wearing just the towel, I went to the door and opened it.

November

I knocked on the door. I was sure I heard him call out as if in surprise.

I knocked again. "Hey, Kale!"

There was the sound of frantic rustling from the other side of the door. What was he doing? I wondered.

"Kale, are you there?" I knocked again.

"Just one moment," he called out, sounding a little out of breath.

Perhaps he was in the middle of something and wanted to be left alone. I was just turning back in the direction of my room, when he opened the door. I looked back, then glanced away at once. Kale stood in the open doorway, with just a white towel wrapped about his waist. In the brief glimpse I caught of him, I could see that his upper body was well toned. Lean, but muscular.

"Is everything okay?" Kale asked me. Now it was my turn to feel uncomfortable just like he had in the bar. I could feel my own cheeks glowing red.

"I brought you this to use," I said, holding out my bottle of shower gel.

He took it from me, his fingers brushing briefly over mine. I glanced at him then away again.

"Are you sure you don't mind me using it?" he asked.

"Not if you don't mind," I said, staring along the landing, anywhere but the knot of abs covering his stomach.

"Thanks, November," he said.

"That's okay," I said, stepping away from the door. I didn't hear his door close and I knew he was watching me walk back to my room. At the door, I glanced back, even though I told myself not to. He was standing in the open doorway, half naked, just like I knew he would be. I kept staring at his blue eyes and nowhere else.

"What time do you want to eat?" he asked me.

"When you're dress... when you're ready," I said.

"Give me five minutes," he said, closing the door.

Back into my room and with my back pressed flat against the door, I couldn't help but notice my heart was racing a little faster than it had been before.

I was waiting for Kale, when he knocked on my door a short time later. I had fully dried my hair now and it hung in thick, blonde waves about my shoulders and down my back.

"Ready?" Kale smiled. He didn't look embarrassed any longer. His confidence had returned. His dark hair looked as messy as always, even though I could see he had washed it. Without a razor, the lower half of his face was covered with a shadow of stubble. It suited him. He still wore the same clothes as earlier, but he had rolled the sleeves of his blue cotton shirt to the elbows and the tails were untucked and hung over the front of his trousers.

"Ready," I said, stepping out onto the landing. The door swung shut behind me.

We headed down the stairs to the bar. No sooner had we reached the bottom stair, I could smell the delicious aroma of roast chicken. The innkeeper glanced up as we entered the bar area. He winked at me, and I looked away. A young girl, no older than about seventeen approached us. She wore a black dress and white apron. The apron was flecked with gravy. Her blond hair was pulled back into a ponytail. The innkeeper's daughter, perhaps?

Smiling, she said, "Follow me."

She led us to a table near the roaring fire. Kale and I took our seats. We both ordered the roast chicken with vegetables.

"Wine?" the girl asked.

Kale glanced across the table at me. I was paying.

"Why not," I said, looking back at the waitress.

I rarely drank alcohol, preferring a nice cup of tea, but tonight, I just wanted to relax. I needed a little something after what had happened to me at the Sacred Heart Church. The waitress went to the bar.

Once she had gone, Kale said, "As soon as I get paid, I'll give you my share of what it cost to stay here."

"I wouldn't worry about it," I said. "You can pay next time."

"Will there be a next time?" he asked.

"Probably," I said, looking into the fire. "We're friends after all, so we will go to other places together, wont we?"

"I guess," Kale said.

The waitress appeared at the table again. She placed two glasses and a bottle of white wine onto the table. As soon as she was gone, Kale poured us both a glass.

He took a sip. "Well, it beats sitting on my own in Macky-D's."

"And staring out of the window," I said, thinking of my favourite chair back home.

"I thought you liked doing that?"

"I used to," I told him.

"What's changed?"

"Nothing," I said, plucking up my glass and taking a sip.

There was a long silence. I looked over to my right and could see the couple I had seen earlier. They were sitting at the table and holding hands. They were married. But they had had problems in their marriage recently and they had come to this out-of-the-way place to spend time together.

"What are you staring at?" Kale asked

"The man and woman at the table behind you," I said. "They've come here to sort the problems out in their marriage."

"How do you know they've had marital problems?" Kale asked, without looking back at them.

"Look at how close they are sitting to each other. Look at how they are holding hands across the table," I told him. "I don't know of any married couple that sits and hold hands while staring into each other's eyes for hours on end."

"You're so cynical," Kale smiled, taking a mouthful of wine. "Besides, they might be newlyweds."

"Look at their wedding rings embedded deep into the flesh of their fingers. They've both put on a little weight since the big day, which suggests it wasn't recently," I smiled back. "And I'm not cynical."

"But how do you know they've recently had problems?" Kale asked.

"Why else come to such a remote place? They want to spend time together, away from others so they have time to talk without interruption," I said, glancing over his shoulder at the couple, then back at Kale. "But he isn't in love with her anymore, but she is still in love with him."

"How do you know he isn't in love with her?" Kale pushed.

"If he truly loved her, he wouldn't have brought her to a place like this. He has money. He's wearing a Rolex watch, wearing expensive shoes and clothes. No such fineries have been lavished on her. If he really loved her and wanted to make the marriage work, he would have taken her somewhere far more extravagant. He would have wanted to spoil her."

"That kind of love only exists in fairy tales," Kale said.

"Now who's being cynical," I said back with a half-smile.

Kale drank more of his wine. The young waitress arrived, placing two plates of steaming hot chicken and vegetables onto the table. We thanked her and she went back to the kitchen. We sat and ate in silence. It wasn't because we had run out of things to say to each other. Kale was the sort of friend I could sit in silence with and feel comfortable. We were just both starving hungry. Food took priority over any conversation that we might have been having.

"Better than cheeseburgers?" I eventually asked, as Kale sat back in his seat and patted his flat stomach.

"Oh yeah," he smiled. "That was good."

I placed my knife and fork down and pushed my empty plate to one side. Kale refilled our glasses and I took another sip. My head felt a little light, but I wasn't anywhere close to drunk. I just felt relaxed. But it probably was due to the effects of the wine that I asked my next question.

"Kale, were you really worried about me like that guy said you were?"

He looked at me over the table, a flicker of firelight in his blue eyes. "Yes," he said.

"Why?" I asked.

"Because you're my *friend*, remember?" he said right back. "Besides, everything else that guy said was nonsense. He was making the whole thing up."

I lifted my glass and drained it. Looking at Kale, I said, "Did you really tell him you thought I was pretty?"

"I was just trying to describe you. Besides, I've told you before I think you're pretty," he said, shifting in his seat as if uncomfortable.

"Have you?" I asked.

"Loads of times," he nodded.

"I don't remember," I pushed.

"I'm sure I have," he said, taking up his glass and drinking the last of the wine. "What about when you thought Morris Cook was staring at you in that garage? I said he was probably looking at you because you were pretty. See, that was one time I said it."

"I'm sure I would've remembered," I said.

"Why would you, things were different back then," Kale tried to explain.

"Different?" I frowned. "Different, how?"

"We had only just met," Kale said.

"More reason for me to remember," I told him, not letting him off the hook. "I'm sure I would remember a complete stranger telling me I was pretty."

"But we weren't like complete strangers, we were friends already..."

"We're friends now, but you said things have changed," I reminded him. "So what has changed?"

Kale took a deep breath as if steadying his nerves. Then, looking me straight in the eyes, he said, "What I mean is… look… when we first met… over the last few weeks my feelings…"

Before Kale had had a chance to finish what he was struggling to say, the woman at the table with the man suddenly shot to her feet.

"You pig!" she hissed. Raising her hand, she slapped the man across the face. It sounded like a gunshot.

"Ouch!" Kale grimaced, glancing back over his shoulder. "I bet that hurt."

The man sprang from his chair, nearly knocking the table and everything on it over. He gripped the woman's wrist.

"Let go," the woman screeched, her bright red lips rolling back in anger. Her lipstick was the same colour as her dress. Strands of her long blonde hair covered her face as she tried to wrestle free of him.

I made to get up out of my chair. Kale placed his hand over mine.

"We're on a break here, remember?" he whispered. "We're not meant to be getting involved."

"But…" I started.

"But Black warned us to keep apart," Kale said. "We don't need to go getting ourselves involved in drunken domestic disputes."

With my eyes still on the couple on the other side of the bar, I slowly sat down again.

"You promised me you were going to finish with *her*," the woman spat. "You told me it was me you loved, not her."

I glanced at Kale. I wanted to say I told you so, but now wasn't the time.

"Sit down," the man hissed. "Everyone is watching us."

"Good!" the woman yelled, yanking her arm free of her husband's grip. "I want them to see what a lying cheat I'm married to. If you don't tell Lorraine to get lost, then I will."

"Please, just sit down, Melinda," the man said. He glanced over at me and Kale, then back at his sobbing wife. He eased her back down into the chair. Part of me hoped she'd hit him again.

"Do you want a divorce…?" she cried.

"No," he tried to reason with her.

"Good, because I would never give you one," the woman snapped.

"Poor cow," Kale said under his breath, turning away, now that the fight had calmed down.

Then, in a flood of tears, Melinda pushed her chair back from the table and stood up again.

Sobbing, she ran across the bar and up the stairs. The man shot Kale and me another quick glance, then left the bar in pursuit of his wife.

I looked at Kale and him at me.

"What were you trying to say before that row started?" I asked him.

"It doesn't matter," he sighed.

Kale

Had the row between the man and his wife saved me from a world of embarrassment? I had just been about to tell November that perhaps my feelings for her had changed – become confused somehow. It had been on the tip of my tongue to tell her that I thought I liked her more than just a friend. But the sudden argument between the woman named Melinda and her cheating husband had broken the moment.

"What were you trying to say before that row started?" November asked me, her eyes never leaving mine. November's bright hazel eyes seemed to see right through me. As if she could *see* into my soul somehow. Sometimes it made me feel uncomfortable, as if she was reading me like she read a crime scene. Sometimes to be looked at by her was nice. But now it just made me feel uncomfortable. I looked away at the dancing flames in the nearby fireplace.

"It doesn't matter," I sighed.

"Tell me what you're thinking," she said, her voice soft.

I couldn't tell her. It would probably spoil our friendship, and I really didn't want to do that. So looking away from the fire and back at her, I smiled and said, "So where do you think you'll be posted to when we leave training school?"

November shrugged as if half expecting me to ask her something else. "I don't know."

"I don't mind where I get sent, as long as it's not that town called the Sunken Shore," I said with a shudder.

"Where's that?" November asked.

"On the furthest tip of the coast," I said. "Apparently, the town is miles away from anywhere."

"You make it sound like some kind of ghost town," November half smiled. But I could see by the way her eyes sparkled in her pale pretty face that I had caught her interest and imagination.

"It might as well be," I said, dropping my voice to a whisper.

"What do you mean?" she asked, leaning in close across the table. I caught the faintest hint of the shampoo she had used on her thick, blonde hair and the soap she had used on her soft skin. It was more intoxicating than the wine. I felt a sudden urge to tell her how crazily happy she made me feel, but instead, I leant back in my chair and said, "I've heard that most of the new recruits sent to the Sunken Shore don't stay long."

"What, they quit the force?" November asked, her eyes shining so bright.

"Some say they just disappear," I whispered. "Never to be seen again."

"Have these disappearances been investigated?" November asked, her practical self as always.

I glanced back over my shoulder to make sure the waitress wasn't standing close by. Then, looking back at November, I said, "Some say there has been a cover-up."

"A cover-up?" November breathed. "By whom?"

"The senior management team. The top brass at force headquarters," I continued to whisper.

"And who told you all this?" November asked.

"I've heard other officers talking about the Sunken Shore too. The rumours are all the same," I told her.

"Well, if I'm to be honest it's just the kind of place I'd like to get sent to," November said, sitting back in her seat.

"Now, how did I know you were going to say that?" I smiled.

"The whole place sounds like one big mystery waiting to be solved," she said.

"It sounds like a whole lot of trouble to me," I told her.

"We might both get sent to this town called the Sunken Shore," November smiled at me.

"I don't think that will happen," I said, not even wanting to hope for such a thing for one moment. Any future disappointment would be crushing.

"Why not?" November asked with a shrug. "You and I would have the mystery of the Sunken Shore solved in no time."

"Black can't seem to bear the thought of me and you texting each other," I reminded her. "You don't think he is going to send us to the same posting once we leave training school, do you?"

"If the rumours are true about the Sunken Shore, then what two better officers to send?" November said, with a half-smile.

"And that's the very reason they won't send us," I said, staring back at her.

"And what's that?" November asked.

"If what the other recruits say is true, our senior officers don't want the mystery of the Sunken Shore solved, they just want to cover it up."

November sat and looked at me as if deep in thought. I looked at how the firelight made her hair shimmer, and how her pink lips looked so very kissable.

I suddenly pushed my chair back from the table and stood up before I let the wine make me say something stupid – something I would later regret. "I think I might just go to bed."

"Really?" November said, sounding a little surprised.

"I'm dead beat," I lied.

"Me, too, I guess," she said, standing up.

Together we left the bar and went to our separate rooms.

November

I woke with a start the following morning. Someone was knocking on my door. Clawing hair from my face where it lay matted and tangled, I groaned and swung my legs over the side of the bed. I padded to the door in my pyjamas. It was barely light outside, and I guessed it must be before 7 a.m. What was the point in taking a break from things if you couldn't even have a lay-in?

"Who is it?" I asked, the side of my face to the door as the knocking came again.

"It's me, Kale."

Trying to straighten my hair, I opened the door a fraction and peered through the gap at him.

"What's the time?" I croaked, eyes still half shut. He looked wide awake.

"Six-thirty," he beamed, bright-eyed.

"You're kidding me," I sighed, just wanting to climb back into bed. My head still felt a little fuzzy from the wine I had drunk the night before.

"I thought we could go for an early morning walk. Build up an appetite for breakfast," he said.

"Why?" I mumbled, struggling to become fully awake. I didn't share Kale's enthusiasm for taking a brisk early morning walk in the freezing cold.

"I thought we could walk down onto the beach and watch the sun come up," he said, taking a flask from behind his back. "And share some of this tea."

"Where did you get that?" I asked.

"That young waitress made it up for me," he said.

"Been working your charms again?" I asked.

"Like magic," he grinned back at me.

How could I refuse? "Give me ten minutes."

"And you might need this," he said, holding up my bottle of shower gel in his other hand.

I snatched it from him and closed the door.

Kale was waiting by the bar at the foot of the stairs. With the collar of my coat pulled up and my hands thrust into my jacket pockets, we made for the door. It was just getting light as we stepped out into the cold. A chill wind blew hard across the fields that stretched away from the small car park. The stars were fading in the sky and a thin ribbon of orange glowed on the horizon where the sun was slowly rising.

"It's so peaceful," I whispered, the soft howl of the wind circling us. "The sky looks beautiful."

"But that doesn't look so beautiful," Kale said, stepping away and heading toward his car.

"What's wrong?" I asked him.

"Someone has pranged my car," he said, bending low and inspecting a dent in the back. "Look at that, can you believe it?"

I looked at the dent that had scratched and removed the paint beneath the bumper of his car. Turning, I began to inspect my motorbike in the light shining through the inn windows.

"What are you doing?" Kale said, straightening up and looking at me.

"Checking to see if my bike has been hit too," I said.

"That thing's a death trap," he said. "People are always getting killed on bikes."

"You're just mad because someone has hit your car and driven off," I said. "It can be fixed. Besides, I thought we were going to sit on the beach and drink tea while we watch the sunrise, not stand out here inspecting your car."

"It's just that..." Kale started, scowling back at his car.

"C'mon," I said, offering him my arm.

He looked back at me. Then, hooking his arm through mine, we made our way in the direction of the beach.

We crossed the barren land before the inn. It was covered in a coarse grass which came up to our knees. The nagging wind bent it to and fro. The sky grew lighter with every step we took in the direction of the shore. As we grew closer to the cliffs ahead of us, I could hear the faint roar of the waves crashing into them. The wind blew my hair back off my shoulders. Arm in arm, Kale and I reached a narrow path that wound its way along the cliff edge. We stopped and looked out across the ocean. The rising sun shone its orange glow off the black churning waves, making them look like molten lava. With my feet close to the cliff edge, I peered down. Giant black waves crashed into the jagged rocks below.

"Let's keep going," Kale said, moving off, his arm still through mine. "We might find a way down onto the beach.

We walked further along the coastal path, and just when I thought we were the only people in the world, I spotted a car parked ahead of us. As we drew closer, I could see a red sports car parked on a flat sandy piece of ground in the distance. The sun cast enough light now for me to see it clearly. The headlights were out, but I could see the outline of two people within the car.

"See, I wasn't the only one mad enough to want to come out and watch the sunrise," Kale said.

The path we were following led us right toward the car. As we got closer to it, I could see the shapes in the front of the car moving around, it looked like two people were making out. I looked away and back out across the ocean, as I didn't want to pry. As we passed along the sand-covered path, Kale nudged me in the ribs with his elbow.

"Hey, look who it is," he whispered over the screech of the wind. "Looks like they made up."

"Who?" I said, shooting a discreet sideways glance at the car. The man and woman we had seen arguing in the bar the night before were in the car. She had her back to us, as the man held her in his arms. They were passionately kissing. He had his eyes closed as he ran his hands through her long, blonde hair. Suddenly, the man opened his eyes and looked over her shoulder and straight at me. Feeling embarrassed that I had been caught watching them kissing, I looked away again. Kale pulled at my arm and we continued along the path.

"I wouldn't have forgiven him so easily," I said as we reached a point in the path where it split.

"Like you said, November, she loves him," Kale remarked, taking the split in the path that led down onto the beach.

"Love has to work two ways," I said. "It can't be just one-sided."

"I guess you can't help who you fall in love with," Kale said glancing at me then quickly away again.

We reached the beach. Kale found a little outcrop of rock that sheltered us from the wind. Unlinking arms we sat down on the sand. I drew my knees up, resting my chin on my hands. I watched the waves rush up the shore, bringing with it stringy lumps of black seaweed. Kale poured the tea. He handed me the plastic cup first. I warmed my hands against it as I took a sip. It was sweet and hot.

"If Black could see us now," Kale smiled mischievously.

"I don't want to talk about him right now," I said.

"So what do you want to talk about?" Kale asked.

I handed him the cup of tea so he could have his share. "I'm just happy to sit and watch the sunrise. Doesn't it look beautiful?" I breathed.

Kale looked out across the ocean. Seagulls squawked as they circled overhead, their white wings shimmering gold in the autumn sunlight. We sat silently next to each other in the sand and drank the tea. When it was finished, Kale replaced the cap on the flask.

"So do you think she is foolish for forgiving her husband?" Kale asked, looking out over the waves and not at me.

"That lady in the car, Melinda, you mean?" I asked.

"Yes."

"It's not for me to say," I said. "But all I know is that I wouldn't want to be in love with a man like that."

There was a short pause. Kale picked up a fistful of sand and let it dribble through his fingers. "What kind of guy do you see yourself falling in love with?" Kale eventually asked.

"I guess I won't know until I meet him," I said.

"Oh," Kale said, sounding a little deflated.

I looked at him. "Are you okay, Kale?" I asked.

"I'm fine," he said, smiling at me, but it looked a little forced. Then springing to his feet, he added, "Come on, let's get back to the inn. I'm starving. That young waitress said there's eggs and bacon for breakfast."

Kale took me by the hand, pulling me to my feet. "You and that waitress," I teased. "You've got a *thing* for her, don't you?"

"I don't have a thing for *her*," Kale said.

"Who then?" I teased further.

"I'll guess I'll let you know when I meet her," Kale sighed, setting off up the beach in the direction of the inn. As we made our way back along the coastal path, I couldn't help but notice that Melinda and her husband had gone.

Kale and I sat at the same table we had the night before. The pretty waitress brought more tea. Kale thanked her, and I kicked him under the table. He blushed. He did like her. I could *see* it a mile off. I doubted Kale would have the courage to ask for her number, despite his sometimes cocksure attitude. She would be a lucky girl if he did. Kale was a cute guy, with abs to die for. I wouldn't mind having a guy like Kale asking for my number. But I knew he only thought of me as a friend, despite him telling the innkeeper I was pretty. But that was good. We should remain just friends. We both had police exams to pass, and neither of us needed any further distractions than the ones that had already come our way. Perhaps that was the true reason Sergeant Black had wanted to keep me and Kale apart? Relationships between police recruits was frowned upon as it diverted our attention away from our studies. But whatever Black's true motive was for wanting to keep me and Kale apart, I would keep my feelings in check for Kale. Besides, I didn't want to make a fool of myself in front of Kale, as I knew he saw me solely as his mystery solving partner and nothing else.

We were still waiting for the waitress to bring our breakfasts when the door to the inn suddenly flew open and the man we had seen kissing his wife came staggering in. His face was white and drawn. Gasping for breath, he dropped into the nearest chair. Both the waitress and the innkeeper came running from behind the bar and stood before the man.

"You've got to help me," he said trying to catch his breath.

"What's happened, Mr. Took?" the innkeeper asked him.

"It's Melinda," Mr. Took panted. "She's had an accident."

"What kind of accident?" the waitress said.

With his eyes bulging, Mr. Took looked at her and said, "Melinda has fallen over the cliff edge and into the sea. I think she's dead."

No sooner had the words left his mouth, Kale and I were on our feet and crossing the bar toward him.

"Where did this happen?" Kale asked.

"Near to where you saw Melinda and me parked this morning," he said, looking at Kale, then at me.

"Go and fetch Mr. Took some water," the innkeeper told the waitress. She did as she was asked as the innkeeper went to the bar and snatched up the phone.

"Tell me exactly what happened," I said, looking at Mr. Took. He sat forward in the seat, his brow covered with sweat despite the cold.

"I think it is obvious after what happened in the bar last night that me and Melinda had quarrelled over some personal matters," Mr. Took started to explain. "But we talked all night, sorting out our differences. Just before daybreak we had found a resolution between us and decided to go and watch the sun come up. It's what people who are in love do, isn't it?"

Kale glanced at me, then back at Took. "Then what happened?"

"It was very cold and Melinda decided that she didn't want to walk, so we drove down to the cliffs in my car," Took continued. "We found a spot which gave us a beautiful view of the rising sun. It was as we sat together, I realised what a fool I had been and how badly I had treated Melinda. So I took her in my arms and kissed her. To my deep joy, she kissed me back and I knew I had not yet lost her. It was then I saw you both stroll past. Melinda was a little embarrassed at being discovered kissing in the car like a couple of teenagers. So we waited for you to pass, then climbed from the car and went and stood on the cliff edge. From that vantage point we watched the sun fully rise. But as we turned to leave, Melinda lost her footing on a loose piece of rock. I grabbed for her, but I was too late, it was like she had suddenly vanished before my very eyes. Peering over the edge of the cliff, I watched Melinda bounce off the jagged rocks, then disappear beneath the crashing waves. I screamed out her name until my throat felt raw. But it was no good. She had gone, swallowed up by the sea."

I looked at him, tears spilling onto his cheeks. "Why not call for help before now?" I asked him.

"I tried," he said, pulling his phone from his coat pocket. "But the damn battery is flat."

Kale took the phone from him and inspected it. Handing it back to Mr. Took, Kale looked at me and said, "It's dead."

I stared at Took. "Why has it taken you so long to get back here? We passed where you had been parked and your car had gone. We were on foot, yet we got back here quicker than you."

"I drove further along the coast, hoping that I might be able to see her," Mr. Took said.

"And you didn't think to stop and ask for help?" Kale cut in. "You didn't stop at a public pay phone?"

"There is no one about in such a remote place and so early," Took said. "And there were no public phones, not that I came across. Look, what is going on here? Why are you asking me all these questions instead of trying to help me and Melinda?"

"The police are on their way," the innkeeper said, stepping away from the bar. "But they could be a couple of hours yet."

"Two hours!" Took snapped, springing to his feet.

"There is no longer a police station in Port Haven," the innkeeper said. "Got closed down due to cutbacks, what, with the credit crunch. The nearest police station is in the village of Sandy Point, but that's not manned twenty-four hours and the first copper doesn't book on duty until nine this morning."

I glanced down at my watch. There was still an hour and a half before that happened. Then it was a good hour's drive from Sandy Point to Port Haven, even on blues and twos.

"This is outrageous," Took barked. "What about the coast guard?"

"They're just volunteers. Like I said, cutbacks," the innkeeper grunted. "The emergency operator is going to try and scramble some together."

"Oh, sweet Jesus," Took said, slumping down into his chair again. "Somebody has got to do something to help my Melinda."

I slid my hand into the back pocket of my jeans and reached for my police badge. I couldn't stand by and not help this man, despite what I thought of him. Kale rested his hand on my arm before I'd the chance to take out my badge.

"You wait here for the police, while me and my friend go back to the cliffs and search for you wife," Kale said. "Should we see the coast guard, at least we will be able to point out the place where you had parked and where you say your wife fell from the cliff edge."

"Thank you," the man said, wiping the sweat from his brow.

Taking me by the arm, Kale led me from the inn. Once outside, I said, "Why didn't you want me to show him my badge?"

"Because in an hour or two, this place is going to be crawling with coppers," Kale said. "And if Black…"

"I don't think we can afford to worry about what Black might think at a time like this," I said. "Melinda Took could be dead."

"Whether Mr. Took knows we're cops or not, it doesn't change anything," Kale said, heading across the grassy scrubland and back toward the cliffs. "There is only so much we can do to help until the police and the coast guard arrive."

Kale started to run and I matched his speed. With the wind screaming up off the sea, we reached the coastal path. We headed in the direction we had seen the car. Even though we ran at a pace, I kept my eyes cast down at the ground.

"That's where the Took's were kissing in their car," Kale said, pointing into the distance. We raced toward it.

Reaching the spot on the sand dunes, I looked at Kale and said, "You go and check out the cliff edge and I'll see what I can find where the car had been parked."

"Melinda Took didn't fall out of the car," Kale said. "She fell over the cliff."

"I just want to take a look," I said, turning away.

Kale

While November headed toward the spot where Mr. Took had earlier parked his car, I went to the cliff edge. The wind flapped my coattails about my legs and I pulled my coat tight. Teetering on the cliff edge, I peered over. I half expected to see the remains of Melinda

Took's body dashed against the black rocks, but there was no sign of her. Mr. Took seemed to be right; the writhing black waves had taken her – as if swallowing her whole. Leaning out over the edge as much as I dared in the nagging wind, I strained to see in both directions along the coast. All I could see was the black and grey jagged rocks. They rose out of the sea like a series of spikes. Anyone who had fallen over the edge would either be impaled on them, or dragged beneath the churning waves of the sea that crashed against them. I feared in my heart that Melinda Took would never be seen alive again. Her death seemed even the more tragic due to the fact that she had, in the moments before dying, patched up her failing marriage. I guessed that the last few months of her life had been unhappy ones, thanks to her husband. I could never imagine myself hurting the person I loved the most in life. But then perhaps November had been right about that too. November had said the night before in the bar as we ate that she could see Melinda loved her husband, but he no longer loved her.

With any hope I might have had in my heart that Melinda Took might yet still be alive fading, I turned in search of November. I stepped away from the cliff edge to find her bent low over the sandy patch of ground where Mr. Took's car had been parked. To watch her was like watching a bloodhound that had found a scent that it refused to let go of. It really was a marvel to watch November at work. It was like I was no longer here. Somehow, November had stepped into a different zone where she could hone in on the clues, tracks, and marks left behind by those who had gone before her. On her hands and knees, she would suddenly see something ahead and spring to her feet. She would drop flat on the ground, where she would inspect in the minutest detail the marks left in the sand. Then, as if charged with electricity, November would jump to her feet again, stooped forward, hands clasped behind her back. I watched from afar as she peered down at the ground, her eyes fleeting left then right. Once more, she would drop face-first into the sand, her nose just inches from the ground as she made her inspection.

As I watched November work, it was like I wasn't even there. I felt as if I had disappeared and all that mattered to her were the clues she searched for. Thrusting my hands into my pockets, I knew that love and romance wasn't ever going to be November's real passion. Solving mysteries is what she loved.

November

    While Kale searched for any signs of Melinda, I hunkered down and stared at the sandy path that led to the spot where the car had been parked. "Be careful where you step," I yelled back at Kale.

    "Don't worry, I won't go over the edge," he hollered.

    "I didn't mean that," I said. "Don't step on any footprints. I can already see that they will be important in solving this mystery."

    Crouching low, I inched my way forward on my hands and knees. When I saw something I thought was suggestive, I stopped and let my fingers brush gently over the sand. I moved slowly forward again. I could see the tyre tracks left behind by the car. There was so much for me to see. It was fantastic. With an excited smile forming at the corners of my mouth, I carried out my inspection of the flat sandy patch of ground where Mr. Took had parked his car. When I had seen enough, I stood and span around. Stooping forward, I retraced the ground I had already inspected and headed toward the cliff edge where Kale was standing. I dropped to the ground so I lay on my front, the tip of my nose almost touching the sand.

"What can you see, November?" Kale asked.

"Shhh," I whispered, letting my fingers glide over a footprint that had been left behind by Took.

Ignoring me, Kale said, "There is no sign of Melinda."

"I doubt very much we will ever see her again," I muttered. When I had seen enough, I sprang to my feet, brushing sand from the front of my coat, then my hands. I looked at Kale.

He matched my stare. "What have you seen?"

"I believe Mr. Took murdered his wife," I said.

"But we saw them kissing, they looked happy enough," Kale reminded me.

"Mr. Took lied to her when he said he was sorry for the mistake he had made," I started to explain. "I suspect he told her that to coax her out to this remote spot. Here he kissed her, told her he loved her. Lulled her into a false sense of security. After we had passed by, I think he murdered her."

"How?" Kale asked.

"Strangulation, perhaps," I said. "It's the only sure way of her not crying out. He would have feared we might have heard her. And there aren't any signs of blood. If he had wounded her, then there is every chance that a trail of blood would've been left as he carried her from the car and threw her body over the edge of the cliff into the sea."

"Hang on a minute, November," Kale said, raising one hand. "How do you know he carried her from the car and threw her over the cliff? You make it sound like you were here when it happened."

"Let me show you what I've seen," I told Kale, heading back towards where Mr. Took's car had been parked. Kneeling again, I pointed down at the sand. "Here are the tyre tracks where the car was parked. See here and here. This is where Mr. Took climbed from his car. The footprints are far too big to be that of a woman's. These would suggest a size ten or eleven shoe. But there are only one set of tracks. Where are Mrs. Took's footprints? There aren't any," I explained. Then, placing my finger into the footprints leading away from the car, I continued. "These prints are deeper than those coming back from the cliff edge. This suggests that Mr. Took was heavier on his way to the cliff than he was when he made his way back to the car. Did he suddenly lose some weight? No, he was carrying something. It was Melinda Took's lifeless body that weighed him down."

"But..." Kale started.

"And look at the return footprints," I said, brushing my fingertips over them. "Mr. Took walked back to the car. Wouldn't he have run? He said himself he was panicked by his wife falling over the edge of the cliff. He said that he was desperate to find help."

"How do you know he walked back to the car?" Kale asked, squinting down at the footprints I was pointing to.

"The distance between them is the same as when he walked away from the car," I explained. "If he had run, the distance between each footprint would be bigger. Not only that, the front of the shoe would have made a greater impression in the sand than the heel. Even when he got back into the car, Mr. Took didn't rush to get help."

"There are no skid marks in the sand, or any signs that he hurriedly made a three-point turn," Kale said, looking down at the tyre tracks. "He slowly reversed back toward the road."

"Exactly!" I beamed. "Are they the actions of a man who has just seen his wife fall over the edge of a cliff and into the sea?"

"But we can't prove any of this, November," Kale said, looking down at the footprints, then back at me. "It's all circumstantial. And by the time the police arrive, these tracks will be long gone, blown away or filled in with fresh sand."

I glanced down at my watch. "We still have about an hour before the police get all the way out to the inn from Sandy Point. Let's go back and tell Mr. Took what we've discovered. Let's see what he has to say to that. We might yet find a more substantial clue to prove his guilt."

Side by side, we raced across the scrubland and back toward the inn.

Pushing open the door, we hurried inside. Took was still seated at the table where we had left him. The innkeeper paced back and forth while the young waitress supplied Took with fresh tea. No sooner had we stepped into the inn, than the three of them glanced up at us.

"Well?" Took said. "Have you found Melinda?"

"No," Kale said, stepping toward him.

I stood next to Kale and looked down at Took.

"Melinda didn't fall over the edge of the cliff, did she, Mr. Took?" I said.

"What do you mean?" he gasped.

"You threw her dead body over the cliff and into the sea."

The young waitress let out a gasp and covered her mouth with her hands. The innkeeper stopped pacing and stood stock still.

"Is this some sort of joke?" Took said, his eyes narrowing as he got up from his chair.

"No joke," Kale said, pushing Took back down into his seat.

"I'll tell you what happened," I said, never taking my eyes off him. "You rowed with your wife last night because you've been having an affair. During the night you tried to convince her that you were sorry and it was her you loved. Before sunrise, and while the rest of us slept, you coaxed her down to the cliffs on the pretext that you wanted to watch the sunrise with her. You kissed her, told her that you loved her, so that she trusted you. We saw you. At first this might have given you cause to panic, but then you saw us stumbling across you as a good thing. You had two independent witnesses who would state you and your wife were very much in love before she died – so why would you have killed her? Once we had passed, you strangled your wife because you knew she would never give you a divorce. She would always be a thorn in your side."

"I don't have to sit here and listen to this..." Mr. Took said, getting up from his chair again.

Kale pushed him back into it.

"Once you had throttled the life from her, you carried your wife from the car, then threw her body over the cliff edge and into the sea. Then, Mr. Took, you casually walked back to your car. I suspect the reason why you took so long to get back here wasn't because you went in search of her further down the coast, but because you needed to get your thoughts together – get into character – before you came bursting into the inn telling us that your wife had fallen to her death," I said.

Mr. Took looked at me and I couldn't help but notice a sudden spark of fear in his eyes. "I don't know what you think you've seen down at the cliffs," he tried to bluster, "but this is all just a fantasy you've created."

Ignoring him, I looked at Kale. "I was wrong last night."

"About what?" Kale asked me with a frown.

"Mr. Took didn't bring his wife all the way out here because he didn't want to spend any money on her," I said. "He brought his wife out to this remote spot because he always intended to murder her here. I suspect he knew that it would take some considerable time for the police to get here. That would give plenty of time for Melinda's body to drift far out to sea and perhaps never to be found…"

"You think you've got it all figured out," Mr. Took suddenly sneered.

I looked back at him and he wore a hateful and contemptuous leer on his face. The true monster was revealing himself.

"I think me and my friend have you all figured out, Mr .Took," I said.

"And even if you have," Took suddenly grinned. "How will you ever prove it? You're just guessing."

I knew Took had murdered his wife, but I just couldn't prove it and that drove me half-crazy with frustration, and he knew it. There was something missing and I just couldn't find that final piece of the puzzle. I looked away from him, his smug expression was starting to anger me.

"And I bet it was you who smashed into my car this morning," Kale said. "Who else could it have been? Yours was the only other car parked here."

"Where was your car parked?" The innkeeper suddenly asked.

"Right out front," Kale said.

"That's a real pity," the innkeeper said. "I don't have CCTV out the front. But I've got a camera out back. I've had to have it fitted for insurance purposes. I got burgled last year. It's only a small little camera. You'd never know it was there. I've got it concealed so I could catch the little buggers who broke in..."

"Shhh!" I said, raising my hand and going to the window. I looked out at the small car park at the front. It was then I realised what the final piece of the jigsaw was. Where was Mr. Took's bright red sports car?

"Where is your car, Mr .Took?" I said, spinning around to look at him.

"Parked out back, of course," he sneered. "You don't think I would park a classic like that out front for all to see. It would get stol..." Then as if realising his mistake, he suddenly clamped his mouth shut.

"Show me this CCTV," I said to the innkeeper.

"Follow me," he grunted. "I never bother to check it. I'd only ever take a look if anyone broke in again."

He led the way around the other side of the bar. There was a small monitor, which was off. The innkeeper switched it on and the screen flickered into life. I could now see the small parking area concealed at the back of the inn. Mr. Took's red sports car was parked there.

"Can you take the picture back?" I asked the innkeeper.

"Sure," he said, pressing the rewind button on a small DVD player tucked beneath the monitor. I glanced up and over the bar. Kale was still standing next to Took as he sat in the chair, his face now drained of all colour. The young waitress stood by the door to the inn.

"What's this?" The innkeeper breathed deeply as if in shock.

I looked down at the monitor, then back at Kale. "You'd better come and look at this."

Kale came around the other side of the bar and stared down at the monitor. The time in the top right-hand corner of the screen read 05:36 hrs of today's date. The car park at the back of the inn was shrouded in darkness but, the image was clear enough to see Mr. Took's gleaming red sports car. Then from the corner of the screen appeared Took. He carried something in his arms. As he got closer to his car and the camera, I could clearly see that he was carrying the lifeless body of his wife in his arms. Her long, blonde hair trailed over his arms like liquid gold. Her eyes were open as was her mouth. Her face looked to be permanently frozen with a look of fear. At his car, Took cradled his wife's dead body in one arm as he fumbled with the door. He opened it, then glancing back over his shoulder at the inn to make sure he wasn't being watched, he forced Melinda's body into the car. He reached inside, and as if she was nothing more than a bundle of old rubbish, he crammed her body out of sight down into the foot well.

"Jesus," the innkeeper whistled through his teeth. "You were right."

Before I'd had a chance to say anything, there was a scream. I looked up to see Mr. Took leap from his chair. He pushed the young waitress away from the door. She fell against the stone wall. In a blink of an eye, Kale bounded over the bar and was chasing after Mr. Took as he fled out the door.

Elbowing the innkeeper out of the way, I raced around the bar and out of the door after Kale. Ahead, I could see Took racing over the scrubland that led to the cliffs. Kale was at his heels. Then, as if in the middle of a game of rugby, Kale leapt into the air, wrapping his arms around Took and bringing him down to the ground. Took began to kick and punch out as Kale wrestled with him. The innkeeper was a big man, but he wasted no time in racing past me and assisting Kale. He pulled Took free as Kale wrestled with him.

"I don't like no trouble at my inn," he said, rolling back his fist and driving it into Took's nose.

I cringed at the hideous crunching sound that followed as blood gushed from Took's nostrils.

"You've broken my nose…" Took cried.

"Shut your mouth!" the innkeeper said as he drove his fist once more into Took's face. Took stumbled backwards, then collapsed unconscious into the grass.

Kale got to his feet, brushing dirt, grass, and sand from his clothes and hair. "Are you okay?" he asked me.

"Fine," I said. "And you?"

"Never better," he grinned at me.

In the distance I could hear the very faint sound of police sirens. I looked at the innkeeper and he looked back at me.

"I don't know what it is with you two, but something tells me that you don't want to be around when the police arrive," he said.

"You guessed right," I said. Would he cover for us? The guy didn't like trouble.

He looked over his shoulder in the direction of the approaching sirens, then back at me and Kale. "I've got the CCTV evidence and I'm sure the police can figure out the rest," he said. "As far as I'm concerned, you two kids just disappeared while I apprehended myself a killer."

"But you know my name," I reminded him.

"Do I?" he winked back at me.

Knowing that he would keep mine and Kale's secret, we turned away. I had only taken two steps, when I took the key to my room from my coat pocket and handed it to Kale. "Grab my rucksack and crash helmet from my room and I'll meet you by my bike."

"Why?"

"I just want to have a word with the innkeeper," I said.

"Okay." Kale ran back toward the inn.

Kale

With the sound of the police sirens growing ever closer, I raced across the patch of scrubland and toward the inn. The door was open and it wailed back and forth in the wind. I had been right; this place was as creepy as hell. I headed into the bar area. The young waitress was standing by the fireplace, a hand to her head. A thick stream of blood trickled through her fingers. I headed for the stairs and November's room, then stopping, I turned back.

"Are you okay?" I asked her.

"I grazed my head against the wall of the fireplace as Mr. Took pushed me out of the way," she said, dabbing the blood away with her fingertips. She seemed to shiver as she looked down at the blood.

"The cut doesn't look deep," I said, taking a step closer to her, yet mindful that November and I still had to escape before the police arrived. The sound of the approaching sirens grew louder with each passing second. I saw a napkin on one of the nearby tables and snatched it up.

"Use this," I said, handing it to her.

She closed her hand around mine. Her touch was almost ice cold. No wonder she had shivered. Perhaps she was going into shock. I looked into her eyes, and where I had only moments before believed them to be a clear blue, they now sparkled hazel in the light from the nearby fire.

"Thank you," she said, looking right back at me. Then, without warning, she leant forward and kissed me gently on the cheek. Her lips were soft and they lingered longer than a simple display of gratitude.

Taking a step backwards, I said, "You're welcome." I pulled my hand from hers, her long, cold fingers brushing one last time over mine.

I turned and headed for the stairs, and as I went I noticed that there was a small slip of paper in my hand. With the sirens close now, I pushed the piece of paper into my pocket and raced up the stairs to November's room.

November

I turned to face the innkeeper. Mr. Took still lay unconscious at his feet.

"Why are you really prepared to lie to the police? You could get into trouble if the truth ever came out. You don't even know me."

The innkeeper smiled. "I think I met your father once. He seemed like a good man. It seems only right that I help his little girl if I can."

"You knew my father?" I breathed.

The innkeeper looked back over his shoulder in the direction of the approaching sirens, then at me. "Go, November, your secrets are safe with me."

"But..."

"Run, before they catch you," he whispered.

Turning, I raced back across the scrubland and toward the inn. I reached my motorbike just as Kale came rushing out into the car park, carrying my rucksack and crash helmet. I took them from him.

"Follow me," he said. "When we've put some distance between here and us, I'll stop."

"Okay," I said.

The wailing sirens were close now. Throwing my rucksack onto my back and putting on my crash helmet, I climbed onto my bike and started the engine. As always, the bike started first time as she roared into life.

"Good girl," I whispered, racing at speed out of the car park and onto the road.

With Kale right behind me in his car, I sped away. I glanced back in the wing mirror just once. The innkeeper was still standing in the field. The burnt autumn sun cast long, black shadows behind him.

Some miles away from the inn, Kale overtook me. We drove for a short time more until Kale pulled in ahead. There was a small picnic area alongside the country road we found ourselves on. I stopped my bike behind Kale's car and climbed off. Together we sat in the sun at one of the nearby picnic tables.

"That was close," I said.

"Do you think the innkeeper will keep his promise?" Kale asked.

"I think so."

"I hope so for our sakes," Kale said. "If Black were ever to find out what we'd got ourselves caught up in..."

"I don't think he will," I said, thinking of the innkeeper and what he had said to me.

We sat in silence and looked out over the rugged hills and valleys that stretched before us.

"I don't want to be picky or anything," Kale eventually said. "But you were wrong."

"About what?" I asked.

"Took didn't strangle his wife in the car like you thought he had," Kale said.

"In a way, I wished he had," I said thoughtfully.

"Why?"

"Because when we saw him in the car, he was kissing Melinda Took's corpse." I shivered.

"A *pervert* as well as a killer," Kale said.

"I don't think he was a perv," I said. "Took was probably pulling his wife's dead body from out of the foot well, when he looked up and saw us. Like I said before, he turned that moment to his advantage, or so he thought."

We sat in silence again. Kale pulled a slip of paper from his pocket. I could see that there was a series of numbers written upon it.

"What's that?" I asked him.

"When I went back to get your rucksack and crash helmet, that young waitress gave me her phone number," he explained.

"I knew you liked her," I said.

Kale let the slip of paper slide from his fingers where it dropped to the ground.

"What did you do that for?" I asked him. "I thought you liked her."

"She's not the girl for me," Kale sighed, getting up from the picnic table and heading back toward his car.

I looked back down at the slip of paper and watched it flutter away on the wind.

"Where are you going?" I called after Kale.

He stopped, turned, and looked at me. "To tell you the truth, I have no idea. But wherever it might be, do you want to come?"

"I'd love to," I smiled at him.

Splitfoot & The Dead Girl

November

Derren Splitfoot made a gagging noise in the back of his throat. He clawed at his eyes as if they were on fire, then collapsed across the table. It was the rest of us in the room who should have been spooked, not him.

I hadn't even wanted to go to the séance, but Kale said he thought it would be a fun idea. I only agreed because it was the first time since leaving the town of Port Haven that I had seen him smile. I had followed Kale across the country for miles. He had said he had no idea where he was heading next, but he'd asked me if wanted to go with him, wherever that might be. I had agreed. So riding my motorbike, I followed him into the night. Despite Kale's cockiness and athletic frame, he could be a puzzle too. He had looked kind of confused as he let that pretty young waitress's phone number slip from his fingers to be blown away on the wind. Why hadn't he kept it? Kale was a good looking guy with the charms to match. Whoever Kale ended up with would be a lucky girl. I doubted I would ever be lucky enough to end up with such a nice guy. Knowing my luck, I'd probably end up with some arrogant chain-smoking jerk who swore a lot. All the things I disliked in a guy. But like I had said to Kale as we sat and watched the sunrise, I wouldn't know who the right guy for me was until I met him. And perhaps, like me, Kale wouldn't know who the right girl for him was until he saw her. Besides, I knew Kale wanted to concentrate on his career for now, and that was probably the real reason he threw that young girl's phone number away. But if I was honest with myself, there was a tiny part of me that was glad he had.

Trying to push thoughts of Kale from my mind, I began to wonder if Melinda Took's body had been found. Had it been washed up on some remote beach further along the shore? I hoped it had. She could then at least be laid to rest and the police would have more evidence against the vile Mr. Took. I pictured him kissing her corpse in the car. It seemed that some people would stoop very low indeed to try and get away with their crimes. I was learning a lot about the dark and cunning side of people. I was starting to understand that there was more than just finding pieces of a puzzle, like footprints, loose strands of hair, and blood splatters. I had to learn how to *see* into people's hearts and how dark they might be. That's where the real truth hid. That's where we kept our darkest secrets – locked away inside of us. Were these killers born evil, or did some event in their young lives turn them toward a path that they found too hard not to follow? And what about the man who had killed my father? What was his reason for doing so? I guess I would only ever find out if I caught him.

I peered ahead, the brake lights on Kale's car glowing red. He was slowing down. Glancing at my watch, I could see that it was just after 1 a.m. We had been driving for hours. The last road sign I had seen was pointing us in the direction of the peak district. I knew that was where Kale's parents lived. I glanced left and right, but there was only darkness. While lost to my own thoughts as I'd blindly followed Kale, I had lost all sense of direction. It was as if I'd been riding on autopilot. Kale stopped his car just ahead. With the engine still running, he climbed from it. The headlights reflected back off a large metal gate that blocked the narrow road ahead. I sat on my bike and watched Kale push it open. As he did, large spots of rain started to fall and splatter against my visor. Shielding his eyes against the rain with one hand, he waved me forward through the now open gate.

Kale

The only place I could think of heading was home. I knew November didn't want to return to Bleakfield yet and neither did I. To go back there would mean we would have to split again – keep apart – as Sergeant Black had ordered us to do. I had no money, so booking into another inn or motel was a no-go. November had already forked out for our rooms at the Hook Inn and I couldn't expect her to pay again. Not because of chivalry, but because I couldn't be a ponce. It wasn't in my nature. I had burnt out my credit cards and had nothing until payday. I could always ask my parents for money – but I wouldn't do that either. I wanted – needed – to pay my own way from now on. I didn't want to be mummy's or daddy's little boy anymore. I wanted to be able to stand tall and proud and on my own two feet for once. That was important to me. I'd never wanted for anything in my life. My parents had always provided everything for me. Anything I'd ever wanted they had conjured up. And now for the first time there was something I truly did want and I doubted my mother and father would be able to give it to me. I wasn't talking about money this time around.

I glanced in my rear-view mirror and saw November riding behind on her motorbike. I looked away again and concentrated on the road that would lead to my parents' house. They were away for Halloween, staying in their villa in the South of France. Both had asked if I had wanted to join them, but I said no, telling them that I wanted to spend the time studying for my police exams. I glanced in the mirror back at November, then front again. I hadn't done much studying; that was for sure. I just couldn't concentrate and it wasn't the mysteries we had come across that had scrambled my brains. It was November Lake who had done that. But I had to get a grip. I had to learn that I couldn't always get what I wanted in life. You couldn't buy love – you couldn't buy a person – and definitely couldn't buy their heart. And that was kind of strange. The most precious thing that anyone could give you – they gave away for free. True love didn't come with a price tag or a sell buy date, or instructions. And perhaps that was the thing I was struggling to understand. There was no manual I could go to and read to find out what to do with the feelings I now had racing around inside of me, in my brain and in my heart. For the first time in my life, my mother and father wouldn't – couldn't – give me what I wanted wrapped up with a shiny bright bow. I couldn't put what I wanted together like those construction kits I had been given for Christmas as a boy. There was only one person who could give me what I wanted and show me how to understand the feelings that now prodded at my heart. I glanced back at November on her bike, then front again. But I sensed that person didn't feel the same.

Over the last few weeks I had solved many mysteries with my newfound friend, but I feared the greatest mystery of them all I wouldn't be solving with November Lake.

Knowing that my mother and father were away and with nowhere else to go, I had decided to lead November back to my home. The place I had grown up. The place where I had everything – but in strange way – it was the one place I had nothing at all. I steered my car up the narrow lane that led to my parents' country mansion.

November

I waited while Kale swung the gate closed. He climbed back into his car and overtook me on the wide gravel path I now found myself on. Slowly, I followed Kale, the sound of wet gravel crunching under the wheels of my bike. Dark rain clouds scudded across the night sky. They drifted apart and the moon shone through. In the silver light I could see what looked like a mansion looming ahead. Vast, neatly cut lawns stretched away on either side of me. Trees swayed in the wind and rain. I remembered Kale telling me that his father was a defence lawyer and was a partner in a prestigious firm. I was now slowly realising exactly how prestigious that firm of lawyers must be.

Kale drew his car to a stop and climbed out. He pulled his coat up over his head and hunched forward. He looked like the Hunchback of Notre Dame as he stood sheltering beneath his coat in the rain. I stopped my bike and climbed off, removing my crash helmet. I looked up at the house and two white pillars were set on either side of the double front doors. The house stretched away to my left and my right, a countless row of windows looking out across the vast rain-soaked lawns like blank eyes.

"Let's not stand out here in the rain," Kale said, fishing a set of keys from his coat pockets.

"This is your parents' house, right?" I asked.

Kale pushed open one side of the wide front door and ushered me inside out of the rain and wind. "Yes," he said, crossing a large circular hallway to an alarm panel on the wall. It had started to emit a chorus of high-pitched bleeps. Kale punched a series of numbers with his thumb and the noise stopped. He turned to face me. I looked past him at the broad staircase that led up into the dark. Kale switched on a lamp that stood on an ornate wooden stand.

"I couldn't think of anywhere else to go," Kale said, taking off his jacket and hanging it on a nearby coat and hat stand. He came across the hall and took mine from me.

"Your parents have a beautiful home," I breathed, looking around at the oil paintings that hung from the walls, the china vases, and deeply piled rugs. "Was this where you lived as a boy?"

"Some of the time," he said, leading me across the hall to another set of doors.

"Only some of the time?" I asked.

"Spent most of my time away at boarding school," Kale said with a tinge of regret. "Only ever came home when the school broke for holidays."

The door opened onto a sprawling kitchen. I could have fitted my poky flat into it ten times over. Everywhere I looked there were gleaming work surfaces, appliances, sinks, taps, tables, and chairs. It all looked too new, like none of it had ever been touched. It wouldn't have surprised me to learn that if anything ever got the slightest scratch it was replaced at once. It was hard to believe that a single meal had ever been cooked here. The kitchen looked like something from a showroom.

"Does anyone ever cook in here?" I asked.

"Sure," he smiled back at me. "My parents have a cleaner, but my mum cleans before the cleaner arrives. Says she doesn't want the place looking untidy for when the cleaner turns up. My mother says it gives the wrong impression."

"So what's the point in hiring a cleaner?" I smiled back.

"Beats the hell out of me," he grinned. "Would you like some tea?"

I glanced down at my watch. It was nearly half past one in the morning. I was tired and cold. Even though, I said, "Okay that will be nice."

Kale filled a kettle that looked as if it had just been taken out of its box. I sat at the long wooden kitchen table and watched him as he prepared our drinks.

"Are you hungry?" he asked, looking back over his shoulder at me. "I could make some cheese on toast or..."

"No, I'm fine," I said with a shake of my head. I got the feeling that Kale was trying to make conversation – idle chit-chat to fill the silences that fell between us.

"Kale, is everything okay?" I asked him.

"Yeah," he said without looking back at me, splashing milk into the steaming cups of tea. "Why shouldn't it be?"

"You haven't been the same since we left that picnic area," I said. "Since you threw away that waitress's number. Why didn't you keep it? I thought you liked her..."

"I didn't like her," Kale cut in, placing the cup of tea he made for me down onto the table. I placed my hands around the cup to warm them. "What I mean is, I didn't like her the way you think I *liked* her."

"Oh," I said, taking a sip of my tea. "I didn't mean to..."

"I know you didn't," he said, stirring his tea with a small silver spoon. I watched Kale from over the rim of my cup and couldn't help but think he was on the verge of blurting something out but couldn't quite find the right words. He looked at me, then away again, down at his tea.

Then guessing I knew what was wrong, I said, "Kale, you know I wouldn't have minded you calling that girl. I wouldn't have got jealous or anything. I know we've spent a lot of time together recently, but I just think of you as a good friend. You don't have to worry, it's not as if I've got the hots for you or anything. It was kind of you to think of my feelings though." I knew deep down that part of what I said was a lie. My feelings for Kale did run deeper than purely friendship, but I could never tell him that. I couldn't bear the embarrassment of letting him know that perhaps my feelings were changing the longer I spent with him, when he thought of me as just his friend. So I buried those feelings deep and the little pang of jealously I suspected I would have felt if he had kept that waitress's number.

"Just friends then?" Kale said, looking at me and I couldn't help but think his smile was forced somehow.

"Just friends," I smiled back, taking another sip of my tea.

"Good," he whispered and looked away.

Kale

Just friends wasn't what I wanted to hear November say, but at least I knew how she felt about me. It saved me from spilling my guts to her only to end up looking like a complete and utter jerk. My stomach knotted like I'd been punched as I heard her say those words, and I had to look away. I couldn't meet her stare. I knew November saw a lot and I didn't want her to see how suddenly crushed I felt knowing that there would never be anything more than just friendship between us. But that was good, right? At least we were friends. Friends stayed friends forever. Maybe if something more had developed between me and November, and it had all gone wrong at some future point, then the chances are that we would have lost our friendship too. But what if things had worked out between us? I pushed that thought away. There was little point in torturing myself.

"I don't know about you," I said, pouring the dregs of my tea into the sink and washing them away, "but I think I'll go to bed. I'm whipped." All I really wanted to do was bury my head beneath my pillow.

"Sure," November said, pushing her chair back from the table. "Where should I sleep?"

With me! Stop it, Kale, I told myself and bit my tongue. "There are plenty of spare rooms," I said instead, leading November from the kitchen.

She picked up her case from where she had left it by the front door and followed me upstairs. I switched on lights as we went. At the top of the stairs I led November along the landing, stopping outside the door of one of the spare rooms.

"You'll find everything you need inside," I said, looking at her. "There is an Ensuite bathroom and shower, fresh towels... and... if there is anything else that I haven't thought of then I'm right next door."

"Thanks," November said, pushing open the door to the spare bedroom. She glanced inside then back at me.

I looked back into her bright hazel eyes that were framed with long black lashes. On tiptoe, November suddenly leant forward and kissed me softly on the cheek. "Goodnight, Kale," she said, stepping into the room, closing the door and leaving me alone on the landing.

With a smile of happiness – or perhaps it was regret – I went to my room, closing the door behind me.

November

I woke and at first I had that horrible feeling of disorientation that you get when you wake to find yourself in unfamiliar surroundings. Remembering that I was at Kale's parents' house, I rolled onto my back and closed my eyes against the bright sunlight that poured through the large windows and into my room. The huge bed had been so soft I couldn't even remember falling asleep the night before. With my eyes shut tight, all I could remember was saying goodnight to Kale and closing the door behind me. Opening one eye, I glanced at my wrist watch that I must have taken off and placed on the small nest of drawers next to the bed. It had gone eleven and I'd slept most of the morning away. I stretched, wriggling my toes beneath the sheets. Swinging my legs over the side of the bed, I went to the bathroom. From below I could hear the sound of pots and pans rattling in the kitchen and music playing. After showering and dressing in jeans and a sweater, I left my room and headed downstairs. I crossed the large hallway and went into the kitchen. Kale was cooking scrambled eggs. The kitchen smelt of toast.

"I didn't think you were ever going to wake up," Kale smiled, piling a mound of scrambled eggs onto two slices of buttered toast.

"Have you been awake long?" I asked, taking a seat at the table and pouring myself a cup of tea from the pot.

"Long enough to take a five mile run, shower, and cook you breakfast," he said, placing a plate on the table.

The eggs looked light and fluffy on the toast.

"You haven't been for a five mile run, you liar," I teased him, sprinkling pepper onto the eggs.

"Okay, two miles," he laughed, sitting across the table from me and watching me eat. "But it's still further than you've run this morning."

"I was so tired," I said, starting to eat my breakfast. Kale was back to his bright and confident self. Whatever the problem had been last night, it had obviously passed. I guessed he had just been tired like me.

"So what do you fancy doing today?" he asked.

"What is there to do around here?" I asked, looking out of one of the many kitchen windows at the acres of fields. "It looks pretty remote around here."

"It is," Kale smiled. "Why do you think I always try and avoid coming back? I thought that perhaps we could test each other for our next police exam and this evening we could go and see Derren Splitfoot."

"Who's Derren Splitfoot?" I asked around a mouthful of toast.

"He's a medium," Kale said.

"Like a psychic?"

"I guess," Kale shrugged.

"I didn't know you believed in that kind of stuff?" I asked, surprised by his suggestion.

"I don't," Kale said, with a shrug. "But this guy comes once or twice a year to the local pub and holds a séance. Usually it's full of old ladies wanting to make a connection with their dead husbands, that sort of thing. But he's meant to be like really good. Some lady my mother knows went to one of his séances and she was really freaked out by it."

"Why?" I asked, my interest in this Mr. Splitfoot growing.

"Well, all these psychics are meant to have some kind of spirit guide, like a Red Indian or something," Kale started to explain. "Anyway, this Derren Splitfoot's spirit guide is meant to be some young girl. Apparently when he gets going, you can hear this girl talking. Some even claim to have seen her."

"It has to be some kind of an illusion," I said.

"Exactly," Kale beamed. "But no one has ever been able to figure out how this Splitfoot guy does it. Until tonight that is."

"What's that supposed to mean?" I asked.

Kale pushed a copy of the local newspaper across the table at me. "See, this Derren Splitfoot, is holding a séance tonight and you're going to figure out how he tricks people into believing they can hear and see this dead girl."

"Now hang on a minute…" I started, raising my hands.

"Go on, November, it will be fun," Kale beamed, that sparkle back in his eyes. "It will be fun trying to figure it out. Besides, this guy is nothing more than a conman. He's got to be. After all, there are no such things as ghosts."

I looked at him across the table, a grin stretched right across his face. It was the first time I had seen him truly smile since throwing away that waitress's phone number. Rolling my eyes and sighing, I said, "Okay, I'll go with you. But if we do figure out how this guy Splitfoot is conjuring up this dead girl's voice – spirit – whatever you want to call it, we keep it to ourselves. A lot of people believe in this stuff. It brings some people a lot of comfort."

"Okay, okay," Kale said, springing up from his chair. "You can help me make a cake."

"Cake?" I frowned. "I thought we were going to revise for our police exams."

"We can do that while we bake," Kale said, rubbing his hands together with glee.

"Why do we need to bake a cake?" I asked.

"Everyone who attends the séance has to take a treat along for the little girl..." Kale started to explain.

"What? The ghost?" I tried not to laugh.

"Yeah, I know, sounds crazy, right?" Kale chuckled. "But this Mr. Splitfoot reckons that the more sweets and treats that are brought the more likely his spirit guide – this dead girl – will come through. She must have had a real sweet tooth when she was alive."

173

"Either that, or Mr. Splitfoot owns a sweetshop," I said. "So the cake is instead of payment?"

"No, you have to buy a ticket as well as taking along sweets and cake," Kale said.

"How much are the tickets?" I asked.

"Twenty pounds each," Kale said.

"Twenty pounds!" I cried.

"I told you he was a conman," Kale said.

"And I guess you want me to pay for you, too?" I asked, knowing that he was skint.

"No, I can pay for myself," Kale said, reaching into a nearby cookie jar. He pulled out a bunch of notes. "My mother's emergency stash – pay the window cleaner, that sort of thing."

"I'm beginning to suspect this Mr. Splitfoot isn't the only conman around here," I said, prodding Kale in the ribs with my finger.

Kale

While I baked the cake, November sat with the textbooks open in her lap and asked me questions about police evidence and procedure. In the background the radio played. When a particular song came on that we both liked, November would put the textbook to one side and we would either sing raucously together or I would chase her about the kitchen table with my flour covered hands. I had never had so much fun studying – if that's what we were really doing. With James Blunt singing *Heart to Heart* blasting from the radio, I managed to ensnare November in my arms. With her giggling and trying to push me away, I flicked flour from my fingers at her. November yelped with delight as I chased after her again, arms out before me like one of those zombies I enjoyed shooting so much in video games.

Trapped in the corner of the kitchen and her hands to her face, I looked at her, and smiling said, "Come here."

"No," she said, shaking her head of long blonde hair. "You'll put flour on me again."

Reaching for a nearby tea towel, I wiped the flour and cake mix from my fingers. "All gone," I said, raising my hands in the air.

"What do you want?" she half-smiled, stepping away from the corner toward me.

When she was within touching distance, I pulled her close. "You've got flour on your nose," I said, brushing it gently away with my thumb.

Giggling at my touch, she looked up into my eyes. "Has it all gone?"

"Nope," I said. "There's a smudge here." I brushed flour from her cheek.

"Anywhere else?" she said, no longer laughing but looking at me.

"Here," I said, one arm about her waist as I lightly brushed white dust from her chin.

"Is that the last of it?" November said, her eyes never leaving mine.

"And here," I said, daring to brush the tip my thumb over her lower lip.

She didn't flinch or move away at my touch, and if I were ever to kiss November Lake, that was the moment. But that moment became two, three, then four. And the longer it lasted, the weaker the spell that had suddenly fallen over us grew, then faded altogether. The music stopped and the silence became deafening.

"Perhaps I should go and clean up properly," November whispered, easing herself from my arms and heading for the kitchen door.

"Okay, sure," I said, my heart racing. I turned back to the cake I'd been making.

November

With my skin still tingling from where Kale had touched me, I raced across the hall. I climbed the stairs two at a time. I headed down the hall and back to my room. Pushing open the door, I darted inside. With my heart racing, I pressed my back against the door and waited for my breathing to level out. What was happening to me? What was I thinking? I needed to get a grip of myself. I had been a heartbeat away from kissing Kale and making a complete fool of myself. I dropped onto the bed.

I felt my cheeks flush hot at the thought of what might have happened if I had actually lost my mind and kissed him. I would've never been able to look him in the eye again out of complete embarrassment. And what would have poor Kale thought? He would have been embarrassed too. I could have ruined everything. I could have ruined our friendship. I sat up on the edge of the bed and felt angry with myself for being so foolish. I usually had more sense. I still had ten weeks or more of training school to get through with Kale. Did I really want to spend those next ten weeks trying to keep out of Kale's way because I'd embarrassed the both of us? Why risk the amazing friendship I had found with Kale, all for a kiss? I must be losing my mind.

I touched my cheek where Kale had wiped the flour away. I slowly let my hand drop back into my lap. And however much I told myself to not be so stupid and to get my feelings in check, I couldn't scrub away how good it felt to be held in his arms, to have our faces just inches apart while he looked down into my eyes, his hands soft against my face. I had never been held like that before. I had never felt feelings like that before.

November, stop it! I told myself, springing up from the edge of the bed. I went to the bathroom where I ran myself a cool shower. Stripping off my clothes, I stepped beneath the water. I washed the flour from my hair and the feeling of Kale's touch from my skin.

Even though I had long since climbed from the shower and put on a clean top and jeans, I stayed in my room. I sat by the window just like I spent so much of my time doing in my rented rooms back in Bleakfield. I looked out across the fields. My intention was to stay in my room until the time came for us to leave for the séance. I hoped that by then, Kale would have forgotten all about what had happened in the kitchen. Kale wasn't stupid and he would've known I was hoping that he would have kissed me. If we were ever going to kiss, that would have been the moment. And the fact that Kale didn't kiss me proved that I was right in my suspicions that he saw me as nothing more than a friend. I know, because I had figured that much of the puzzle out!

So I sat in the room at the window until the sky had turned indigo in colour. As I debated whether now was the right time to leave my room, there was a knock at my bedroom door. I got up from my seat. The door swung open and Kale stood in the doorway.

"Are you hiding from me?" he asked, trying hard to sound carefree.

"Erm... no... I had a shower then fell asleep on the bed," I lied. I couldn't tell him I was too embarrassed to leave my room and face him.

Kale took another step into the room. He wrung his fingers anxiously together. "Look, November, I just wanted to say that I'm sorry if I..."

"You have nothing to say sorry for," I said, snatching up my jacket and heading past him toward the door. "Let's just forget it."

"If you're sure," I heard Kale say as I left the room and headed along the landing and toward the stairs.

Kale

How I wanted to dig a big hole and climb inside it. I knew that November had been hiding in her room in fear of me taking her in my arms and contemplating kissing her again. Why had I been so stupid! I had made her feel so uncomfortable that she had shut herself away in her room all afternoon. What sort of a friend would do that? Some friend I was turning out to be. And in my heart I knew that if I didn't get my feelings under control – and soon – I might scare November away altogether. She had made it perfectly clear to me on more than one occasion that all she wanted from me was friendship and I had to respect that.

I followed November from the room and along the landing. She had asked me to forget what had happened in the kitchen, so I would. I didn't want to cause her any more embarrassment or discomfort. I just wanted to have a fun evening with my *friend*.

Friend! Friend! Friend! Friend! Friend! May as well drum it into your thick skull, Kale, because that's all she wants. So get over it, I told myself.

Reaching the hallway, I picked up the cake I had made, which now sat in a plastic container on a nearby chair. I opened the front door and we stepped out into the cold. It had started to rain again. "Shall we go in my car?" I asked her. "There's no point..."

"That will be fine," November cut in, heading quickly through the rain to my car.

I pressed the key fob with my thumb and the locks on the doors opened. November climbed inside. I got in beside her and started the car. We drove in silence down the gravel path and back out onto the narrow road.

"So you finished the cake?" November asked. I doubted she was really interested in my baking skills. She was just trying to fill the silence.

"Yep," was all I could think of saying.

"It smells good," she sighed.

"Let's hope Mr. Splitfoot's spirit guide thinks the same, or this is going to be one big waste of time," I said.

We reached the pub just before seven. It wasn't a long drive from my parents' house and eventually the conversation between November and I had become a little less difficult. By the time I'd parked the car in front of the pub, it was like the embarrassing incident in the kitchen had never happened. I felt a massive sense of relief that my schoolboy behaviour hadn't damaged our friendship.

Together we ran the short distance through the rain and into the pub. The name of the pub was stencilled above the old oak door, but most of the lettering had fallen away. The only visible word remaining was *Steam*. Above this was a painting of a black steam train, thick clouds of smoke spewing from its dark funnel. I pushed the door open. November slipped under my arm and I followed her inside. There was a group of people gathered at one end of the bar. Most of them were elderly and each of them clutched a Tupperware box or cake tin under one arm. November saw them too. Glancing back at me, she smiled.

"Want a drink?" I asked, taking one of the ten pound notes I had found in the cookie jar from my pocket.

"Just a Coke," November said.

The bartender was a bony man with a bald head, and glasses that sat perched on the end of his nose. From over the top of them he eyed the cake box under my arm. "With that lot, are you?" he said, nodding in the direction of those gathered at the other end of the bar.

"Yes," I said then ordered our drinks.

"You don't look the type," the bartender said, pushing two Cokes across the bar at me.

"Type for what?" November asked him.

"A séance," the bartender said.

"It's just a bit of fun," I told him.

"Is it?" the bartender said, cocking an eyebrow at us then turning away.

I handed one of the Cokes to November and picked up the other. I turned away from the bar and stopped. Someone was leaving the pub I thought I recognised.

"What's wrong?" November asked me.

"I thought I just saw someone…"

"Who?"

I looked a November. "I thought I just saw Constable Jon Harris leaving the pub."

"Harris?" November frowned. "Isn't he one of the tutors from police training college? What would he be doing all the way out here?"

"More importantly, what if he saw us and tells Sergeant Black? We're not meant to be together," I reminded her.

With Coke in hand, November went to the door. Pulling it open she peered out into the dark. "I can't see anyone," she said. November closed the door and came back, standing at my side. "You could've been mistaken. And besides, he might not have seen us. And even if he did, why would he tell Sergeant Black? It's only us who knows that we shouldn't be together."

"You know what training school is like," I sighed. "If he did see us together all the way out here, then he might think that there is something going on between us and spread gossip. That would soon get back to Black."

"Well there is nothing going on and it was probably someone who looked like Harris," November said, "Let's try not to worry about it."

"I guess," I said thoughtfully. I did only get a fleeting glimpse of the guy as he left the pub, so perhaps November was right and I was worrying about nothing. I took another sip of my drink.

November

Standing at the bar next to Kale, I looked at the gathering of people who had come to take part in the séance. They were mostly pensioners. Perhaps Kale was right and they did come to such events to try and make contact with those they had lost. I guess there comes a time in our lives when we've lost more people close to us than who are still alive. I had lost my father, but I knew that no psychic with a sweet tooth would ever be able to raise him from the dead. It was just a lot of tricks and nonsense and that's what Kale had wanted me to prove. Most psychics used a stooge who passed amongst the crowds gathered before a séance or reading. The stooge would engage some in conversation, telling some heart-breaking story of how they had come to the séance in the hopes that a connection might be made with a person who had died. The stooge would casually ask others who it was they hoped the psychic was going to make contact with. What did Aunt Mildred look like? I bet she was a sweet lady. She loved to knit, did she? How wonderful. Married to Brian, who passed just a month ago, how tragic.

Just like Kale had said, nothing but a big con, but who was I to judge? I suspected I might see how the trick was done, but as I had said to Kale, I would only share that secret with him. As I stood and sipped my drink and watched the group, I saw a man come from a narrow passageway beside the bar that I hadn't noticed before. Just like the others, the man carried a plastic box under his arm. He was younger than the rest in the group, about thirty-five, and wore a dark suit as if he was attending a funeral. He was thin in the face with a neatly trimmed goatee beard. He caught my eye and smiled. I glanced away, fearing he might think I was watching him. From the corner of my eye, I could see him heading across the bar toward me and Kale.

"What have you brought?" he asked, eyeing the box Kale had under his arm. "Cake, is it? Thought as much. That's why I made cookies. Thought I'd do something different." The stranger pulled the lid back off the box he was holding. I caught a sudden whiff of almond cookies. They did smell delicious. What a waste. No little girl would be eating them tonight. He replaced the lid but it hadn't fastened securely. The lid was open all along one side of the box. I was just about to point this out to him when he started talking again. "I've never been to a séance before. Have you?"

Kale shook his head and opened his mouth, but before he'd had a chance to say anything, the man started to talk again. "No? Ah, well. I've heard this Mr. Derren Splitfoot is meant to be rather good. Some say sensational. I've heard rumours that his spirit guide – a little girl named Alice – actually talks, and some say they've even seen her. I hope the rumours are true."

"Why?" I asked as the man paused to take a breath.

"Because I'm hoping she will be able to make a connection with my dear wife. Susan loved children. Never had any of our own. Susan sadly died before that happened."

"I'm sorry to hear that," Kale said.

"Kevin Barker," the man said, holding out his hand.

"Kale Creed," Kale said, taking his hand and shaking it. "And this is my friend, November Lake."

Nice one, Kale, I thought. Now the stooge knows our names. Kevin Barker, if that was his real name, was obviously the stooge. He would now start asking us questions and feed the answers back to Mr. Splitfoot. God, it was all so easy.

"Pleased to meet you," the stooge said, taking hold of my hand.

I smiled. Now what could I see about this man. I could see plenty. I saw the splashes of water first on his sleeve.

"Your sleeve is splashed with water," I said, taking my hand away.

Barker looked at it. Drops of water glistened up his right sleeve. "Rain," he said, looking at me. "It just never stops."

"I know; it's awful," I said, playing along. There was so much more I could see, but I would save that for later.

"So who are you hoping to connect with tonight?" Barker asked us.

"No one special. What do you do as a living?" I asked, changing the subject completely.

Barker's eyes narrowed. The question seemed to take him off guard in some way. "I'm a jeweller," he said. "I have my own shop in Chesterfield."

"Do you have a business card?" I asked. I doubted if Barker was really a jeweller. He was really employed as Splitfoot's accomplice.

"Why do you want my business card?" he asked.

"I was hoping you might be able to give Kale discount when he comes looking for a *ring* in the near future." I looked at Kale coyly and fluttered my long eyelashes.

Kale looked at me numbly. "A ring?"

"Oh, I see," Barker smiled, reaching into his jacket pocket and looking at Kale. "Thinking of popping the question, are we? I do have a lovely range of engagement rings." Barker held out a small white card. I took it from him.

"Engagement?" Kale said as I inspected the card.

It looked genuine. So perhaps Barker really was a jeweller and moonlighted as the psychic's stooge? I placed the card into my pocket.

Barker looked at Kale. "So, are you hoping to connect with someone special tonight?"

"I don't know anyone who's dead," Kale said, shrugging his shoulder.

"Then why are you here?" Barker asked, baffled.

Before Kale had a chance to answer, a bell was jangled behind us. I looked back to see the bartender standing at the entrance to the passageway. He was holding a small brass bell in his hand.

"Those of you who are here for the séance, if you would like to follow me," he said, turning and disappearing into the passageway.

I looked at Kale and he looked back at me. Kevin Barker followed behind as we made our way down the passage and toward the room where Derren Splitfoot awaited us. On my right I could see two doors fixed into the passageway wall. One had *Ladies* written above it, and the other *Gentlemen*. At the far end there was another door, which was open. The group of elderly men and women shuffled inside.

Kale

In the centre of the room there was a large round table. It was covered with a white cloth. The lights in the room had been switched off. The only light came from a candle positioned before a man sitting at the head of the table. This I guessed was Derren Splitfoot. Behind him was a closed window and rain beat against it. On the opposite side of the room was another table, this was smaller. On it, those in the group had placed the cakes and the sweets they had brought for Splitfoot's young spirit guide. I put the cake I had made on it. Kevin Barker brushed up against me as he placed the box of cookies he had brought with him onto the table. I noticed that the lid was open and I caught a whiff of almonds.

I went back to the large table and sat down next to November. Barker sat in the spare chair on the other side of her. Including Splitfoot, there were thirteen of us gathered around the table in the near dark room. I guessed the darkness added to the whole illusion and gave camouflage to the trickery that was about to take place. I looked at November, who was staring up the table at the psychic. The light from the solitary candle before Splitfoot lit up his face in a gold and orange glow. It was Halloween all right, and he was the pumpkin. His face was plump and round and his eyes were small and dark. Bags hung beneath them in deep folds. He had thin, wispy, black hair that hung from the side of his head like rattails. The room fell into a hushed silence. The bartender appeared from the shadows and passed around a scarlet sack made from velvet. The old men and women gathered about the table placed ten and twenty pound notes into the bag as it was handed to them by the bartender. Was he part of the scam, too? I wondered.

The bag reached me and I took two twenties from my pocket and placed them into the bag. I paid for November. Okay, it was money I had taken from the cookie jar in my mother's kitchen, but it was the least I could do. After all, November had paid for me to stay at The Hook

Inn back in Port Haven. I handed the bag to November and she, in turn, handed it to Barker. He placed his money into the bag and then handed it to the bartender. The bartender left the room, closing the door behind him. I glanced around and could see that the door was the only way in and out of the room, apart from the window in the wall behind Splitfoot, and that was closed too. If a little girl really was going to appear, she had to be in the room already, and I didn't believe in ghosts any more than November did.

The room was so silent I could hear the howl of the wind as it bashed against the side of the ancient pub. Then when the sound of my own heartbeat had become almost deafening, Splitfoot spoke.

"Welcome," he said. His voice was soft, calm – almost soothing. "Please join hands around the table."

I felt November's slender fingers curl around mine.

Stop it, Kale!

My other hand was suddenly gripped. I looked left to see one of the elderly ladies had taken hold of my hand. Her hair was snow white and her face lined with age. She winked at me and I gently squeezed her fingers with mine. I glanced to my right again and saw Barker take hold of November's free hand with his left.

Splitfoot raised his head slowly. Seeing that all of our hands were joined, he said in that dreamy voice, "Whatever happens, please don't break the circle. To do so might break the connection with Alice. It might scare her."

He was good. This was going to be worth every penny of my twenty pounds. Splitfoot let his eyes close and he slowly tilted back his head. I could hear his breathing and it sounded laboured, like he had just taken a long run. The flame before him flickered, threatening to go out, then swelled with light again.

"Are you there, Alice?" Splitfoot said in that oh-so soothing voice. "Come out of the shadows if you are there, Alice. There is no need to be afraid. The people gathered around this table have come to connect with you. You have no need to fear them."

The flame flickered again as if caught in a draught. Splitfoot lowered his head, but kept his eyes closed.

"There you are, Alice," Splitfoot whispered. "I can see you now."

I felt the old woman grip my fingers again. I glanced in the direction Splitfoot was facing but couldn't see anything other than shadows.

"Hello, Derren," I heard someone whisper. The voice was soft like that of a child. A young girl.

Although I knew this had to be some kind of an elaborate hoax, my skin still turned cold with gooseflesh. I glanced at November and she hadn't taken her eyes off Splitfoot for one moment.

"Thank you for coming through tonight, Alice," Splitfoot whispered.

I watched his mouth to see if he was doing some kind of ventriloquist act and throwing his voice.

"You're welcome, Mr. Splitfoot," the little girl's voice came again.

Splitfoot's lips didn't move once. In fact, the girl's voice sounded as if it had come from behind me. I glanced back over my shoulder. Was there a secret recorder hidden? Did Splitfoot always say the same lines so they matched what had previously been recorded by a young niece or friend onto a recorder of some kind? I glanced again at November and she was still staring at Splitfoot at the other end of the table.

Splitfoot spoke again, his voice barely a whisper, eyes closed, and facing front. "Have you brought anyone over with you, Alice?"

"Yes," she answered, her voice now coming from the other side of the room. The old man sitting across from me glanced back, just like I had done. A murmur fluttered around the table.

"Please remain quiet," Splitfoot insisted. "Alice scares easily."

And so did the old woman sitting next to me as she squeezed my hand tighter still.

"What is the name of the person you have brought over with you?" Splitfoot asked Alice.

The candle flickered again. There was a sudden waft of Kevin Barker's almond cookies, followed by what looked like the shadow of a young girl go running around the outside of the table toward Splitfoot.

Kevin Barker suddenly shot to his feet, almost dragging November from her seat as he still gripped her hand in his.

"No!" Barker screamed, letting go of November and throwing his hands to his face. "I can't breathe! Somebody help me! Somebody open the window."

I heard chairs falling backwards in the gloom as the others sitting around the table got to their feet. The candle suddenly went out, throwing the room into complete darkness. I felt November let go of me and spring away.

"November!" I called out.

I span around, and with my hands outstretched before me, I felt for the wall. With fingertips brushing against it, I searched for the light switch. The room was flooded with the sound of screaming. I could hear a man crying out that his eyes were burning. I didn't know if it was Barker or not. My fingers felt the light switch and I turned it on. Spinning around, I immediately scanned the room for November. She was standing by the window, which she had now opened. But instead of looking back into the room, she was staring out into the night. Barker dropped back down into his chair, sucking in mouthfuls of cold air that now blew in through the open window. The others who had gathered in the room for the séance were huddled together and staring back at the end of the table where Splitfoot had once sat. He was slumped back in his chair, his face a devilish scarlet in colour. He was clawing at his eyes. Splitfoot made a hitching – rasping – sound in the back of his throat, then slumped forward onto the table.

November leapt away from the window. She gently eased him back in her arms. She pressed the tips of her first two fingers against his neck in search of a pulse. Then looking up, she said, "Someone call the police."

"The police?" the old woman who had been sitting next to me said. "Don't you mean an ambulance, my dear?"

"It's too late for an ambulance," November said. "Mr. Splitfoot has been murdered."

November

"Murdered?" those gathered in the room muttered as one.

Kale looked across the room at me, eyes wide. I waved him over. Pulling him close, I whispered into his ear.

"Okay," he said. Kale crossed the room and helped Kevin Barker to his feet. He was still gasping for breath. Kale put his arm around him and led him from the room. I looked at the others, who stood staring at me.

"This room is a crime scene and I think we should all leave until the police arrive," I told them. Without argument, they shuffled out of the room, and a few of the more curious old ladies glanced back one last time at Splitfoot's dead body draped across the table.

One of the old women stopped at the door as I tried to usher her through it. She looked at me and said, "Do you think the ghost, Alice, murdered him?"

"Let's wait and see what the police say," I smiled at her, leading her out into the passageway.

I watched her trundle away, then looked back into the room. I switched out the light and closed the door behind me. Instead of following the others back into the bar area, I stood outside the door and waited. It happened sooner than I thought it would. I heard movement in the room I had just left. Taking a deep breath, I gripped the door handle, then flung it open. I switched on the light. The man Kale had mistaken to be our colleague Constable Jon Harris stood at the table, leaning over Splitfoot's corpse.

Like a rabbit caught in a set of headlamps, the man glanced back at me and I could see how Kale had believed this stranger to be Jon Harris. There was a resemblance. Both had greasy hair, wore glasses, and had pimples on their foreheads. The man turned and headed for the open window. I leapt across the room, pulling him back through the window and onto the floor.

"Stay down!" I hissed, driving my boot into his chest.

He cried out in shock more than pain. At that moment, Kale shoved Kevin Barker back into the room.

"What is the meaning of this?" Barker demanded. He was no longer gasping for breath.

"Sit down," I said.

Kale shoved Barker into the nearest chair and then stood with his back against the door so he couldn't escape.

"Up," I said, reaching down and yanking Barker's accomplice to his feet. I pushed him down into the nearest chair.

"I haven't done anything wrong," the stranger spat.

"And neither have I," Barker insisted.

"You murdered Mr. Splitfoot," I said, looking across the table at him.

"Ridiculous," Barker sneered. "There isn't a mark on him. He had a heart attack. It's obvious. He was hardly a picture of health."

"And that's what you wanted us to believe," I smiled knowingly at him.

"If what you say is true, how did I murder him?" Barker dared me.

"You poisoned him," I said.

"Poisoned him!" Barker scoffed. "I didn't go anywhere near the man. Why, you are my alibi. I was sitting next to you the whole time. If I'd got up and moved, you would have known about it, as I was holding your hand. In fact, I was taken ill myself when Splitfoot died. I was ten feet away or more, gasping for breath."

"And that's how you planned to get away with murder," I said. "How could you have possibly murdered a man you were sitting ten feet from?"

"How? Tell me!" Barker insisted.

"You set the trap before Mr. Splitfoot even entered this room tonight, before any of us entered the room," I said.

"This is just a waste of my time..." Barker snapped, standing up. Kale pushed him back down into the chair. I glanced down at the young man sitting beside me, head hung low, then back at Barker.

"At first I thought you were a stooge working for Mr. Splitfoot," I started to explain. "But I was wrong about that. You came from the passageway that led to this room. When you shook my hand, I noticed the right sleeve of your jacket was wet with splashes of water. Rain water."

"I told you *that*," Barker sighed.

"It was rain water," I said. "But why wasn't the rest of your jacket wet? If you had just come from outside, you would have been wet all over. Only your arm had got soaked through with rain. Therefore, I figured that you had perhaps stuck just your arm outside. I didn't know why at that time. But there were splashes of candlewax too on the sleeve of your jacket. And when you took my hand at the start of the séance, I could feel lumps of wax on the palm and fingers of your left hand."

I went around the table, took hold of his wrist, and showed him the patches of dried, flaky wax.

"That could have come from anywhere!" Barker insisted.

"Really, Mr. Barker?" I smiled. "We no longer live in the dark ages. I presume you have electric lighting in your home."

"Of course," he sneered at me.

"I've only seen one candle tonight, and that is this one," I said, pointing to the candle standing on the table before Splitfoot's dead body. "When I entered the room and saw the candle, I knew you had handled it prior to us entering the room. At that time I still suspected that you were working in cahoots with Mr. Splitfoot. But why had you blown the candle out? Why would you have done that?"

"I didn't blow the candle out," Barker cut in.

"The wax on the palm of your left hand would suggest you did," I said. Then cupping my left hand around the wick of the candle, I blew as if blowing out a flame. "You blew out the candle just like I have demonstrated, and your hand became flecked with wax. You couldn't risk any splashing down onto the table or you might have raised Splitfoot's suspicions that the candle had been tampered with. But why switch the candle, and who did you give it to? But I will get back to that in a minute. As I sat in the room and watched Splitfoot start the séance, and with the spooky girl's voice, your heartbeat didn't even twitch. Even when you started to scream, claiming that you couldn't breathe, your heartbeat stayed the same. I should know."

"How would you know a thing like that?" Barker mocked me.

"As I held your hand, I had my forefinger resting against your wrist, Mr. Barker. As some might say, I had my finger on the pulse," I smiled at him. "I, therefore, knew that your panic attack was just a charade. But I still couldn't figure out why. I still believed that you were working with Splitfoot, and at the climax of the séance, you broke out in some kind of fit to divert the attention off those gathered in this room from Splitfoot so he could conceal how he was deceiving his guests.

"You then asked for the window to be opened so you could catch your breath. Knowing that you weren't really short of breath, I knew that you must have had a motive for wanting the window open on such a cold and wet night. So I went to the window and opened it. At the same time my friend Kale turned on the lights, illuminating the ground outside. I could clearly see fresh footprints in the wet ground beneath the window. Someone had been standing outside – and very recently. Then I thought of your wet sleeve and the candle switch. And I suddenly knew how you had done it. You had come into the room and blown out the candle that was already here. You then passed that through the open window to your waiting accomplice and replaced it with another. And that's why you wanted the window opened again, so when we had all left the room, your accomplice could climb back through the window and switch the candles back again.

"But who was your accomplice? Not anyone in the room. And then I thought of the man Kale had seen leaving the pub, who he mistook to be a colleague of ours. I was curious to know if my friend was right, so I went to the door of the pub and looked in both directions along the road. There was no sign of any man, because that man had slipped around the side of the pub to this window where you were waiting to pass him the candle."

Barker looked at me from across the room. He swallowed hard. As if gathering his composure he said, "Why would I want to swap the candle? I thought you said I had poisoned Splitfoot."

"The poison was in the candle," I said.

Barker laughed out loud and clapped his hands together. "Now I know you are truly mad," he said. "I never saw Splitfoot eat the candle. It's right there. Look!"

I glanced at the candle, then back at Barker. "It was the almond cookies that gave you away."

"Cookies?" Barker blustered. "What are you talking about?"

"When cyanide crystals are burnt they give off an odour similar to that of almonds," I said. "When you showed Kale and me the cookies in the pub, you were careful not to close the lid. You wanted the room in which the séance was being held to smell of almonds. Just before you started to scream, and just before Splitfoot died, there was a strong whiff of almonds in the room. But it didn't come from the cookies you had made, but from the flame reaching the cyanide crystals you had hidden in the candle. That's why you needed to switch the candle. And I suspect when the remains of the candle are forensically tested, traces of cyanide will be found."

"And where would I get cyanide crystals from?" Barker said, knowing deep down that he had been caught.

"You told us that you were a jeweller," I said, fishing his business card from my pocket and holding it up. "Cyanide crystals are used in your profession to guild gold. You would have access to such crystals. So before coming here tonight, you placed the crystals into the candle. You snuck into this room before the séance, switching the candle that was already here with your own. You passed the other out of the window so it could be replaced later – something you wouldn't be able to do yourself. When the candle burnt down and reached the crystals, it flared brightly for a moment, emitting a strong whiff of almonds. That was your cue to throw a panic attack and ask for the window to be opened. You knew that Splitfoot would inhale most of the poison as the candle stood directly before him, but you couldn't risk contaminating the rest of the room – or yourself. The open window offered ventilation and a way for your accomplice to regain entry to the room once we had left. I know that you killed Splitfoot and I know how. But what I don't know is why?"

I looked at Barker. He stared back at me, eyes bulging.

"It's not true," he said.

"Stop it! Stop it!" his accomplice suddenly cried out. "Just stop, Kevin. She knows what happened. She knows we killed Splitfoot."

"Shut it, Peter!" Barker hissed at him.

"It's over, Kevin," Peter said. "It's over."

A heavy silence fell over the room. I didn't break Barker's stare once. Kale stood directly behind him, guarding the door.

"Splitfoot was a fraud," Peter suddenly said. "He killed my sister Claire. My sister was married to Kevin."

"Shut up!" Barker tried one last time to silence his brother-in-law.

Peter turned his attention from Kevin and looked at me. "Claire was in a car crash two years ago. My six-year-old niece died in that crash. It was an accident, but Claire blamed herself. Then six months ago she saw an advert in the local paper. It was for one of Splitfoot's séances."

"I told her not to go," Kevin suddenly spoke up. His anger seemed to have suddenly left him at the mention of his wife and dead daughter. He looked deflated, lost, and haggard. "I told her no good would come of going to a séance. They're run by frauds just like Splitfoot who prey on the vulnerable. But he didn't care as long as he got paid. So Claire went to one of his séances, and just like tonight she heard the voice of that little girl, Alice. But that was our daughter's name too. Claire believed that she had been visited by our daughter. It drove Claire half insane with anguish. Her guilt intensified from that day on until she took her own life. Splitfoot knew the harm he had caused, but he didn't stop.

He carried on tricking those poor people like me who have lost the ones they loved most in this life. Someone had to stop him. That person was me. I wanted to send him to join the spirits he claimed to be able to speak to."

Kevin stopped talking and lowered his head. He had given up. The fight had left him.

I took no pride in catching this killer. But sadly that's what he had become. His grief had driven him to despair, just like grief had driven his wife Claire to Derren Splitfoot.

As I struggled to find the right words to say, Kale suddenly stumbled forward as the door was pushed open. Kale straightened as two uniformed police officers came into the room. I didn't recognise either of them, but the officer who stepped into the room behind them was all too familiar. My heart sank.

Sergeant Black looked at me, then at Kale. His face was pale and his eyes burnt with fury.

"You two, my office first thing tomorrow morning," he barked, jabbing his finger at us. "Get yourselves back to Bleakfield on the double before I have both of your badges."

"But..." Kale started.

"Don't mess with me, Creed," Black warned him with a dismissive shake of his head. "Both of you get out of my sight, right now."

Without another word of protest, both Kale and I left the room.

Kale drove me back to his parents' house. Not one word passed between us, although I could think of a thousand things to say. This was my entire fault and Kale was going to get busted off the force because of me. We pulled up in front of the giant mansion once again. I looked at Kale and he back at me. I think we both knew our fate. Come nine o'clock tomorrow, we were both going to be kicked out of police training school.

Before climbing from his car and onto my bike, I said, "I'm sorry, Kale."

"What for?" he frowned.

"For getting you into this," I said.

"I got myself into this," he half-smiled. "I didn't have to come looking for you."

"So why did you, Kale?" I asked. "You never did explain."

Kale stared at me for a long moment, like there was something he needed to say. But at the last minute, he changed his mind and simply said, "It doesn't matter why. I just did."

I pushed open the door to climb out. Kale suddenly gripped my arm. I looked back over my shoulder at him. "What?"

"You never explained how Splitfoot created the sound of that girl's voice and how she appeared in that room."

"I couldn't figure out how he did that," I said, climbing from the car and closing the door behind me.

The Mystery of November Lake & Kale Creed

November

I stood in my bathroom and stared into
the mirror fixed above the sink. I was wearing
my police uniform. The silver numbers shone
from the shoulders of my tunic. For how much
longer would I be wearing them? I wondered. I
was sure to be busted out of the police force
today. Sergeant Black had demanded that we
attend his office at training school for 09:00
hours. I glanced down at my wristwatch. I had
just an hour. One last hour wearing my police
uniform. My stomach clenched at the thought of
leaving the force. Becoming a police officer was
all I had wanted to do since my father's death.
His killer had never been found and it had been
my dream to join the police force so I could solve
that puzzle. I wanted to get my hands on the
murder file and carry out my own investigation
into my father's death. I knew in my heart that if
I read that file I would figure out who had
murdered him. But now that dream was going to
be taken away and with it any chance of finding
the killer. I wiped away the tears stinging the
corner of my eyes, then fixed my hair up in pins,
tucking it beneath my police hat. I left the
bathroom, stepping into my lounge. I looked at

the hundreds of newspapers piled high on the floor. I picked up one of the newspapers. My father stared back out of it. He was dressed just like me, in his police uniform. ***Detective Inspector Thomas Lake – MURDERED!*** The headline screamed in thick, black letters.

"I'm sorry for letting you down, dad," I whispered, brushing my fingers over his face.

I placed the newspaper back onto the pile. I couldn't bear to look at that picture. But it wasn't just my dad I had let down, it was me, too. I had made a promise not only to him, but myself that I would find out his killer's identity. I had planned to do it for the both of us. I turned away. I couldn't look at his picture knowing I had failed him. With those tears building in my eyes again, I sniffed them back and left my rented room. I couldn't very well stroll into Sergeant Black' office with tracks of black mascara running down my cheeks. He would think I had gone in search of pity and I didn't want that. I had brought this situation upon myself. There was no one else to blame other than me. I should have stayed away from Kale like Sergeant Black had warned me to do. But I hadn't been able to. Why not? It wasn't just because we worked so well together. There was another reason I had been unable to put distance between us. And deep in my heart I knew what that reason was, however much I tried to hide it. God, what a mess. I had fallen in love with a guy who didn't feel the same way about me and I was about to lose the job I needed if I was ever to keep the promise I had made to my dad.

With those tears threatening again, I climbed onto my bike and headed through the rain toward training school.

Kale

I straightened my tie and stood back from the mirror. Running my fingers constantly through my messy-looking hair, I jutted my chin out and inspected it for any patches of stubble I might have missed while shaving. I wanted to look my best. I wanted Sergeant Black to see that I was a good copper and worthy to stay in the force. I couldn't get kicked out. Not today. Not ever. The thought of doing so and having to go back to my mother's and father's house with my tail between my legs made my heart sink. I wanted to do something for myself. I had wanted to make my own way in life without their help. I wanted to prove to them – to myself – that I could make something of my life without their constant help. In my heart I knew that I could've never wished for better parents. They had given me everything – they had given me too much. I could just carry on taking from them but I wanted them to be proud of me. I wanted to do something special with my life that would make them proud. And in my heart I knew that's why I had wanted to be a copper. It stood for something, didn't it? To be able to protect and help those in society who could least help and protect themselves, was something to be proud of. That's all I had ever wanted to do. And working with November I was starting to believe that I was doing something worthwhile with my life. For the first time I was doing something that would make my parents proud. So the thought of having to return home and tell them I had failed – been kicked out of training school for failing to obey orders made my heart ache. I could see the look on their faces already and it made me wince. But that wasn't the only reason my heart ached as I put on my tunic for the last time. I knew that once I'd been kicked off the force there was little chance I would ever see November again. There was no way Sergeant Black would get rid of November. She was way too bright. She was going to make a brilliant police officer. She would stay and I would go – go back home. Maybe that was for the best. The best for me. In my heart I doubted I could really stay friends with someone I had fallen in love with. It would hurt too much being around her knowing that she didn't feel the same way. So perhaps being kicked off the force was the best thing to happen. It would force a break between November and me. My heart was already breaking, so perhaps if some distance was put between November and I, those breaks would slowly start to heal?

I left my bathroom and waded through the discarded cheeseburger wrappers and empty Coke cans that littered my room. My PlayStation was still set to pause where I had sat up all night playing. I had been unable to sleep. I picked up the hand controller from off the sofa and hit the play button. A zombie lurched forward on the screen, its eyes wild and blood red. I shot it straight in the face.

"Take that, Black," I smiled to myself and turned off the machine.

I left my flat, darting through the puddles to my car. I climbed inside and headed toward training school.

November

Two uniformed officers stood on either side of Sergeant Black's office door. The officers' backs were so straight I feared that their spines might just snap at any moment. I sat on one of the chairs in the sterile-looking corridor. I looked up at the officers but they just stared straight ahead like mannequins. I looked down at my watch. 08:56 hours. Where was Kale? He daren't be late. Please, Kale, hurry up, I prayed. I didn't want him to get into any more trouble than he was already in. I sat nervously strumming my fingers against my knees. There was a sound of footsteps and I glanced right. Kale was heading down the corridor toward me. He looked so smart in his police tunic. He carried his police helmet under one arm and with his free hand he tried to straighten his wayward hair.

He dropped down onto the seat next to me. "I'm not late, am I?" Kale sounded out of breath.

"No, but you've cut it pretty fine. Where have you been?" I asked.

"Killing zombies," he smiled at me.

Although he smiled, I could see that he was nervous. We both were.

I looked at him and he stared back at me.

"November, I just wanted to say whatever happens today I want you to know…" Before Kale had a chance to finish whatever he wanted to say to me, Sergeant Black's office door swung open.

We both shot to our feet. Black nearly filled the open doorway. His grey hair was swept neatly back from his brow and his light blue eyes looked sharp. The silver buttons down the front of his uniform gleamed like stars, as did the toecaps of his boots.

"Lake and Creed, in my office," he snapped.

We stepped inside and he closed the door behind us. Black walked around his desk and sat down. Both Kale and I stayed standing, our backs now as straight as the officers who stood outside. Several beige coloured folders lay open across the desk. Black thumbed through them, then looked up at us.

"So whose bright idea was it to disobey the order I gave both of you to stay apart?" Black asked, the tone of his voice brusque.

"It was my idea," I cut in.

"No, it wasn't, it was my idea," Kale said. "I texted you first, remember?"

"You two really don't understand how much trouble you are in, do you?" Black said. "Or is it that you both just don't care? It doesn't really matter who did what to who or when or where. I know what you've both been up to."

"I'm not sure I understand," Kale said.

I really hoped he wasn't going to start getting cocky with Black. With the mood Black looked to be in, I wouldn't be surprised if he started bouncing Kale off his office walls.

"Let me refresh both your memories," Black barked, picking up one of the files and tossing it across the desk at us. Sheets of paper flew from the files and fluttered about the room like giant butterflies. "What about the priest – Father Rochford?"

How did Black know about that? Who would have told him? Who could have known?

"A dangerous criminal who was already wanted for kidnapping and imprisoning young girls ends up dead himself at the foot of some well."

"Dead?" I gasped.

"We didn't kill him," Kale cut in.

"I didn't say you killed him," Black snapped back at Kale. "But you let him get away and he must have slipped and fallen down that well and broke his neck."

"He didn't get very far then," Kale said.

Black shot to his feet and pointed one long finger at Kale. "Don't push your luck with me, Creed. Thanks to you two I've had the Superintendent all over me like a rash all last week. Instead of having a break over Halloween, I've spent my time combing the countryside looking for you two and trying to limit the damage you've caused."

"Damage?" I frowned. "All we wanted to do was help."

"Help!" Black scoffed. "What planet are you from, Lake? You walked away from the scene of a murder. You left an innkeeper to explain to the police how that woman Melinda Took was murdered. You had a duty to stay and explain how that woman had been killed. But instead you went running for the hills with your boyfriend."

"Kale isn't my boyfriend," I reminded Black. "We're just friends."

"I couldn't give a toss if you're a pair of identical twins!" Black roared. "You're both finished!"

My heart began to beat faster. I glanced sideways at Kale and the colour had left his face.

"What does finished mean?" I asked Black although I suspected I already knew the answer.

"It means you two are being separated permanently," Black said. "After this meeting, Creed, the two officers outside will escort you back to your room here at training school. You will gather your belongings together and then report to Superintendent Cooper at Force Headquarters first thing tomorrow morning. You will finish the rest of training there."

"But headquarters is miles away..." Kale said, glancing first at me then back at Black.

"That's the whole point," Black cut in.

"What about November?" Kale asked.

My stomach was somersaulting with anxiety.

"Lake will stay and finish her training here," Black said.

"But..." I started. I was grateful that neither Kale nor I was being kicked out of the job, but I didn't want Kale to be posted miles and miles away. We would never see each other again.

"No buts, Lake," Black scowled. "This is the last chance saloon for you two. You're nothing but trouble when together so you're being split up. I don't think you realise how lucky you two are."

"How's that?" Kale asked. "I'm losing my best friend, aren't I?"

"Well, start making some new ones, Creed, because from this moment on, if you two so much as share the same breath of air, you're both off the force. No more chances. There were some who didn't want to give you this chance. This was my idea to save both your arses. I only did it because I happen to think you are both good officers. Probably the best recruits I've ever had. But you're both trouble when together. Not only are you going to mess things up for yourselves, but for me and the rest of the force, too. Creed, go away to headquarters, keep your head down and become the great cop you're meant to be."

"But..." Kale started, glancing sideways at me again.

"Take it or leave it, Creed, your choice," Black said. "But what will your folks say when you arrive back home? Isn't your dad some hotshot lawyer? He's not going to be very proud, is he?"

Kale dropped his head. He looked crushed.

I wanted to reach out and take his hand in mine. I wanted to tell him everything was going to be all right.

"And what about you, Lake?" Black asked, dragging me from my heartbroken thoughts.

"What about me?"

"Didn't you say at your interview that the reason you wanted to join the police was so you could investigate your father's murder?" he said.

I lowered my gaze and nodded.

"You're not going to investigate anything claiming unemployment benefit," Black warned.

I didn't want Kale to be sent away. I didn't want us to be split up. But I didn't want to be kicked off the force either. I had a promise to keep to my father.

"So do we have an understanding?" Black asked, his voice calmer now, some of the anger gone.

Both Kale and I glanced at each other in the same moment.

"Stay and find your father's killer, November," Kale smiled at me. "You'll never find true happiness unless you do."

"And what about you?" I whispered, fighting the urge to reach out and touch him one last time.

"I'm going to go and make my mum and dad proud of me," he smiled, but I could see no happiness in it.

Slowly he turned and left the room. He closed the door without looking back. I could feel those tears building in my eyes again. I didn't want Sergeant Black to see them. So I lowered my head.

"I know it seems hard," Black said, taking his seat again. "But it's for the best, trust me."

Could I really ever trust the man who had just sent my friend away?

As if being able to read my mind, Black said, "You'll make new friends. I know you're trying to prove a point..."

"What point?" I glanced up at him.

"Your father was a great cop, November, and I guess you feel you've got something to prove," Black said. "But I can't cut you any slack. If you really want to help find your father's killer one day, keep your head down and stop looking for trouble. We all want to find the person who killed your dad."

"So what happens now?" I whispered.

"Take the rest of the day off," Black said. "Come back tomorrow. Things will seem a little better then. It will be a whole new day. A whole new start for you. Forget about Creed."

I turned and opened the door and without looking back, I left the office.

Kale

The two uniformed officers escorted me to my room just like Sergeant Black said they would. Both stood in silence and watched me pack my belongings together. What choice did I have but to leave? I could have refused to go, but then I would've been sacked. What then would I have done? Hung around Bleakfield in the hope that one day November might change her feelings for me? What was the point? Black was right, I should go to headquarters, keep my nose out of trouble, pass my police exams, and become the bloody good copper I knew I could be. With my kit bag thrown over my shoulder I let the two officers, who flanked me on each side, lead me silently to my car.

I threw my kit bag onto the backseat, climbed in, and drove away from the training school for the last time. I looked back in my rear-view mirror? Why? Because perhaps I hoped I would see November Lake one last time. I looked front again and headed for my rented room in Bleakfield.

It was still raining when I pulled up outside. I went in and started to pack. I rented the flat furnished so there was very little of my own stuff to box up. I spent the rest of the morning cleaning out the old cheeseburger wrappers, pizza boxes and Coke cans. When I had the flat looking like it had the day I first moved in, I called the letting agent and said that I was leaving and would post the key back through the letterbox. I ended the call and looked down at my contact list. November's number sat staring back at me.

Should I text her one last time to say goodbye? My thumb hovered over her number. Instead of texting, I deleted her number from my phone and left my flat. With my belongings jostling about on the backseat, I drove away from the kerb at speed, my vision blurred where tears had suddenly gathered.

And as I drove away, I couldn't help but think that perhaps I should have found the courage to tell November how I felt about her, even if she didn't feel the same. But that moment in time had been lost forever and there was no point in ever going back.

November

With my arms wrapped about me, I made my way through the wind and the rain to my motorbike. I had made a detour to my room in the training block, hoping that I might see Kale one last time. But the door to his room was open and his stuff was gone.

Climbing onto my bike, I started the engine. With it ticking over, I pressed down hard on the accelerator to drown out the sound of my sobs. At that moment I hated Sergeant Black. He had torn me and Kale apart – he had ripped my heart out. I didn't want to stay without Kale. Training school wouldn't be the same. I wanted to be able to go on solving mysteries with Kale. But there was one mystery I would never solve if I walked away from training school and the police now. And Black knew that. Black knew that I had to stay if I wanted to help find my father's killer. But what about Kale? He had left not knowing how I truly felt about him. How had I let him leave without me telling him how I felt? Did it really matter that he didn't feel the same? Why hadn't I found the courage to do so? Would it be something I would regret for the rest of my life, just like I would regret throwing away the chance of keeping my promise to my father?

With my head thumping and heart aching, I rode out of the car park and headed to my flat. Rain lashed against my visor, making visibility almost impossible. I turned slowly into my street, drawing to a stop at the pavement outside my rented rooms. I killed the engine. As I removed my helmet, I saw a huddled figure sheltering from the rain outside my front door. My heart began to race.

"Kale!" I yelled, racing through the rain toward him.

At the sound of his name, Kale looked up. He ran toward me. We threw our arms tight about each other, our faces cheek to cheek.

"Why did you come back?" I whispered in his ear, tears and raindrops running down my face.

"There is something I need to tell you before I go," Kale whispered back.

"There is something I need to tell you, too," I said, looking into his eyes.

"Is it about some kind of mystery?" Kale smiled through the rain at me.

"The greatest mystery of all," I said, taking his hand in mine. I led him to my front door. Smiling, we stepped inside.

What happened between us in my rented rooms was our mystery. And only Kale and I would ever know how we solved it.

November Lake

Teenage Detective (Book 3)

Coming Soon!

About the author:

Jamie Drew is the author of the 'November Lake: Teenage Detective Series'. Just like, November Lake, Jamie Drew has been a real police officer and has solved many crimes and mysteries in real life.

Jamie Drew now writes full time and is currently working on further 'November Lake' mysteries.

You can contact Jamie Drew by emailing: LakeNovember@aol.com

11614191R00128

Printed in Great Britain
by Amazon.co.uk, Ltd.,
Marston Gate.